THE SHIP
of
LOST SOULS

W9-BON-889

THE SHIP of LOST SOULS

1

by Rachelle Delaney

Grosset & Dunlap
An Imprint of Penguin Group (USA) Inc.

GROSSET & DUNLAP
Published by the Penguin Group
Penguin Group (USA) Inc., 375 Hudson Street,
New York, New York 10014, USA
Penguin Group (Canada), 90 Eglinton Avenue East, Suite 700,
Toronto, Ontario M4P 2Y3, Canada
(a division of Pearson Penguin Canada Inc.)
Penguin Books Ltd., 80 Strand, London WC2R 0RL, England
Penguin Group Ireland, 25 St. Stephen's Green, Dublin 2, Ireland
(a division of Penguin Books Ltd.)
Penguin Group (Australia), 250 Camberwell Road,
Camberwell, Victoria 3124, Australia
(a division of Pearson Australia Group Pty. Ltd.)
Penguin Books India Pvt. Ltd., 11 Community Center,
Panchsheel Park, New Delhi—110 017, India
Penguin Group (NZ), 67 Apollo Drive, Rosedale,
Auckland 0632, New Zealand
(a division of Pearson New Zealand Ltd.)
Penguin Books (South Africa) (Pty.) Ltd., 24 Sturdee Avenue,
Rosebank, Johannesburg 2196, South Africa

Penguin Books Ltd., Registered Offices:
80 Strand, London WC2R 0RL, England

If you purchased this book without a cover, you should be aware that
this book is stolen property. It was reported as "unsold and destroyed"
to the publisher, and neither the author nor the publisher has received
any payment for this "stripped book."

All rights reserved. No part of this book may be reproduced, scanned,
or distributed in any printed or electronic form without permission.
Please do not participate in or encourage piracy of copyrighted materials in
violation of the author's rights. Purchase only authorized editions.

Text copyright © 2009 by Rachelle Delaney. Map illustration copyright © 2010
by Fiona Pook. Illustrations copyright © 2012 by Penguin Group (USA) Inc.
First published in Canada in 2009 by HarperCollins Canada. First published in
the United States in 2012 by Grosset & Dunlap, a division of Penguin Young
Readers Group, 345 Hudson Street, New York, New York 10014. GROSSET &
DUNLAP is a trademark of Penguin Group (USA) Inc. Printed in the U.S.A.

Library of Congress Control Number: 2011043287

ISBN 978-0-448-45777-2 (pbk)   10 9 8 7 6 5 4 3 2 1
ISBN 978-0-448-45776-5 (hc)   10 9 8 7 6 5 4 3 2 1

ALWAYS LEARNING   PEARSON

For my family

CHAPTER ONE

"You there! Get away from that!"

Scarlet McCray had known the crime could land her in deep trouble. For an instant, she'd even considered not going through with it. But then, she'd never been one to let consequences stop her from wreaking havoc, even if the consequences included having one's limbs lopped off. So why, she'd reasoned, start now?

This time, however, after the deed was done and she found herself staring into a merchant's bloodshot eyes of rage, it occurred to her that she might have gone too far.

"Why you . . . you'll pay for that!"

Not that she regretted it. Not one bit. No, this just meant she'd have to run faster.

"Blasted little scalawag. I'll tear you limb from—"

Scarlet didn't stick around to hear the plan. With an innocent shrug and a tip of her cap, she took off sprinting through the streets of Port Aberhard. A hand reached out to stop her, but she twisted and slipped to the left. A King's Man moved to block her path, but she ducked out of his reach and ran on, dodging a pack of pirates and hurdling a barrel of rum, pumping her arms as the thud of her heart began to drown out the voices of her pursuers. She knew this routine well and was content to let the port town blur into shapes and smells, light and shadows. She liked it better that way.

Scarlet McCray could find her way around Port Aberhard bound and blindfolded. She knew it as well as she knew her own worn boots, her crew, and the ship they called home. Port Aberhard looked the same, smelled the same, and felt the same as all the other port towns on all the other islands. Its red dirt roads teemed with ruddy merchants reeking of pipe smoke, loudmouthed pirates drawn to the tavern like compass needles to magnetic north, and King's Men sweltering under blue wool coats, their brass buttons winking under a tropical sun. Smells of fried conch, sweet seaweed, and sour rum clung to the humid air, mingling with the scent of spices from inland forests.

The port towns even sounded the same—grumbling pirates, clipped orders from King's Men, and gleeful cries from cabin boys on leave from the ships they worked on.

But most important was the feeling a person got walking through the ports all over the islands. It was an unnatural feeling. A downright unsettling feeling. The pirates blamed it on the spirits of the Islanders, a people killed by the King's Men in their hunt for treasure. The King's Men declared it to be the feeling of untamed wilderness. Others called it dark magic. Voodoo. No one could agree on exactly what caused this feeling, but neither could they deny its existence. And some islands had it worse than others. Much, much worse.

Scarlet herself had long ago stopped trying to find an explanation for the chill that made her toes curl and her ears tingle every time her crew docked in port. But it never left her—especially not when she was running for her life.

She'd just glanced over her shoulder to see how far she'd outrun the merchant when a sudden wind swept in from the docks and lifted the cap off her head, sending her tangled black hair tumbling down her back. "Scurvy!" Scarlet cried, flailing her arms in an attempt to catch her cap. But it rolled over her shoulder and along the road. "Not now!" She did an about-face, ducked low to snatch it up, and kept running. Leaving the cap behind wasn't an option, for where would she be without her disguise? In a boatload of trouble, that's where.

Soon she came upon a suitably dank and shadowy alley and dove inside. She found a decent hiding spot behind a mound of old crates and crouched there, hugging her knees, hoping the merchant and his helpers hadn't closed in when she'd nearly blown her cover. If they found her, they'd turn her in to the King's Men for punishment. And supposing they discovered that the skinny, dark-eyed boy in ragged trousers and an old gray coat was actually a twelve-year-old girl? That would absolutely scuttle.

Anyway, hers had been a valiant crime as far as crimes went. She'd do it again in an instant, no hesitation. Just fifteen minutes ago she'd been slinking along between the docks, looking for a shiny, green lime or a stray doubloon to pocket, when she spotted a merchant with a great big cage full of birds. Having always been partial to winged things, she approached and instantly felt her stomach turn when she realized what kind of birds the merchant was selling. Only one island creature had such beautiful, ruby-red feathers, marked by a single band of blue and green on each wing.

The Islanders had called them "aras." They'd nearly been killed off completely a few decades ago when the King's Men first invaded the islands to harvest exotic wood and spices and send them back to greedy King Aberhard. The birds' beauty had been their undoing. As soon as the King's Men arrived, they began to blast them out of the sky, then ship their red feathers back to the Old World in overstuffed canvas sacks. Rumor had it that every night, King Aberhard rested his big, greasy head on a pillow stuffed with ara feathers. The thought made Scarlet's blood simmer.

But that wasn't even the worst of it. Old Worlders of all kinds, from spice merchants and wood cutters to plantation owners and pirates, soon descended on the islands as well, hoping to get in on the pillaging and plundering, especially if it unearthed a bounty of precious jewels. The native Islanders, who'd lived in leafy huts and tended garden plots on the islands for hundreds of years, watched with increasing alarm as these pale, brisk men invaded their homelands and spread Old World diseases among them. Islander numbers fell as hard and as fast as the trees around them, and one particularly deadly plague, known as the Island Fever, was rumored to have killed them off completely.

Scarlet hated that story. It made her stomach ache just as badly as the story of the aras. For perhaps the thousandth time, she wished she could have done something to save them.

And so, when she saw the merchant's cage nearly overflowing with the rare red birds, Scarlet wasted no time in committing her crime of passion. She marched right up, grasped the doors of the cage with both hands, and yanked them wide open.

The aras needed no instructions. Out the doors they flew, a long, red ribbon streaking across the sky toward the jungle and hopefully home.

Home. Scarlet bit her lip as she watched them, and for a moment she forgot that she was a criminal, being sized up by a seething merchant with bloodshot eyes and bared teeth . . .

"Stop the boy!"

Tucked away in her hiding spot, Scarlet heard the merchant and a few other men run past, boots crunching on gravel. She let her breath out in a whoosh, then grinned. She'd saved some powerless creatures and made life a little more difficult for the gluttonous, overdressed Old Worlders. Wishing every day could feel so productive, she stood up and dusted off her grimy trousers. Now she'd just sneak out, find her crew, and regale them with the tale of her daring adventure. Maybe it would inspire them in their own mission. They were, after all, in dire need of inspiration.

She stepped out of the alley, blinked in the sunlight, and headed back toward the docks, pulling her cap down low over her eyes, just in case.

A new ship had docked in port—a great big schooner

with Old World flags quivering in the silver afternoon sky. Passengers stumbled from its deck to the dock, looking stunned and grateful to have both feet on firm ground. Most were King's Men, smoothing the wrinkles in their coats and trousers. But two of the travelers, neither one in uniform, stood out against the crowd. One—middle-aged and fat with a shiny scalp—studied a compass. But it was his companion who drew Scarlet's attention: a smallish boy around her age, staring slack-jawed at the busy port before him.

She knew right away what had brought them there. These days, sailors lay anchor in the islands for one reason alone: to search for treasure. Around the time the Island Fever had begun to rage—some seven or eight years ago—one of King Aberhard's underlings began to speak of a treasure he'd come upon. Unfortunately, the man—Admiral Something-or-Other—perished of the fever himself before he got around to explaining exactly what the treasure entailed. But he had captured the curiosity of the king, who promised a hefty reward to whoever found the mysterious thing. Even now, years later, boatloads of pirates, merchants, and King's Men flocked to the tropics, practically drooling at the notion of unearthing the treasure. Most even enjoyed the mystery surrounding it—at first, anyway.

Scarlet studied the boy, noting his tailored coat and stiff, shiny boots. His companion's clothes were slightly more weathered. She wondered how the boy would fare in this part of the world. The islands, rife with drunkards and thieves and generally unsavory types, didn't exactly cater to children and their notion of fun.

Maybe . . . she squinted at the sun, still high overhead. She had a good hour before she had to meet her crew. She could follow these two, just for a bit, to find out what they were about. Children didn't arrive in port every day, and Scarlet knew it was her duty to check this one out.

The boy's traveling companion, maybe his father or some other relative, was pointing to the tavern and patting his protruding belly. Hungry, of course; they'd probably eaten little but hardtack since leaving the Old World. And judging by their tailored coats and stiff, shiny boots, they were more accustomed to dining on roast duck and buttery pastries than gnawing on the rock-hard biscuits that passed as dinner on board a ship. The boy was smoothing down his sandy-brown hair and adjusting his cuffs as if the tavern might have a dress code. Scarlet snickered. The only clothing requirement in port was a sturdy pair of boots, spacious enough to house at least one dagger.

She waited a moment after the pair marched into the tavern, then slipped inside herself. One good thing about the port towns was that the pirates and King's Men who inhabited them were so busy eyeing one another, hoping to catch the other in some wrongdoing, that they didn't notice much else. They rarely noticed stray children wandering around. Unless, of course, those stray children let themselves get spotted while, say, releasing animals in danger of extinction. Scarlet reminded herself to keep a lookout for the merchant with the bloodshot eyes.

The boy and his companion claimed two rickety

wooden chairs on either side of a table sticky with rum, and the boy, looking ravenous, stared around him, eyes unblinking. Scarlet scanned the dim room, barely half full of sailors at this time of day, and slunk along the wall to a dark little nook not far from their table where she could stand for a while without being noticed. The tavern owner gave the newcomers' well-dressed figures a once-over, then hurried into the back with promises of fresh fish.

"After a good meal," the older man was saying, "we'll reconvene in our boarding house and discuss plans for tomorrow." He spoke with an educated accent and an air of authority that Scarlet decided would drive her mad after a day or two. "I'm going to ask Captain Noseworthy about hiring a small sloop to take us there. We'll have to find a few trusty shipmates to join us for navigational purposes—men who won't take off with the . . ." He lowered his voice. "The you-know-what."

Scarlet leaned toward them. She'd bet her front teeth she knew what! But everyone and his monkey had a theory about where the treasure was hidden. Could these two really know any better? She listened closely.

"Do you think," the boy said as he tried to find a clean spot on the table to settle his elbows, "that these men are real pirates, or do you think they just read the stories and dress up like them?"

The older man shushed him, and Scarlet stifled a guffaw. Real pirates? This one had obviously never set foot off the Old World. No wonder his eyes were so wide.

"Quiet, Jem. Don't say anything that might get you stabbed. Now look, I think it would be most useful if tonight you reviewed the botany journals I gave you. You're going to need to identify everything from *Mondatricus triceriaptus* to—"

"Yes, Uncle Finn," the boy named Jem said with a little groan, as if he'd heard this a hundred times before. Scarlet frowned. She wouldn't know a *Mondatricus triceriaptus* if one tripped her and sat on her. Nor did she know what it had to do with the treasure. "But I'd much rather—"

Just then, their fish arrived, and the two tucked in, barely surfacing for air as they devoured every morsel on their plates in concentrated silence. Once finished, they paid and stood to leave. Scarlet followed, for she, too, had business to get back to.

Outside, she trailed Jem and his uncle until they rounded the next corner and stepped into another dim alley, at the end of which stood a ramshackle boarding house. Scarlet was about to let them go on their way when she saw a strange sight: a shadow—no, two shadows—pressed up against the alley wall, frozen and silent, waiting. This didn't look good. Shadows in a dark alley almost always meant bad news. Scarlet was about to call out a warning when a hand clamped down on her shoulder and spun her around, knocking off her cap. "Gotcha!" a gruff voice proclaimed, and she found herself face-to-face once again with her favorite merchant.

The man started at the sight of her long, dark hair. For a moment he softened his grip on her shoulder, as if unsure what to do. Then he seemed to remember something—probably the sight of the aras streaking across the sky—and he dug his tobacco-stained fingers into her skin again. "So the little thief's a girl, is he?" The merchant shook his head and sneered.

Scarlet squirmed under his grip. "Um, *she*," she said, scanning the alley for an escape route as best she could without making it too obvious.

"Heh?" The fury faded from the merchant's eyes, replaced momentarily with uncertainty.

"She," Scarlet repeated, buying herself some more time. "You said, 'So the little thief's a girl, is he?' And that would make *he* a *she*. See?" There was a big stick nearby—if she could just reach it, maybe she could pound him senseless.

"Oh."

"Hm. Pronouns. Tricky things." Ah. A ladder. Even better. It seemed to reach up to the rooftop of the building on her left.

"Er. I . . ." The merchant now looked thoroughly confused.

"Right. Think about that for a while." With a few swift motions, Scarlet squirmed out of the man's grasp, stomped on his right foot, booted his left shin, and made a dive for the ladder as he keeled over, swearing. She scaled the rungs like a monkey, pulled herself up onto the roof, then ran to another edge so she could look down on the alley where she'd last seen Jem and his uncle.

They'd disappeared and so had the two mysterious shadows. Scarlet ran farther along the edge of the roof and saw several figures ducking down another lane. Two of them seemed to be struggling, accompanied by the unmistakable clang of pirate cutlasses.

"Scurvy!" Scarlet cried, for now it was too late to help them. If only she'd been quicker or more aware of that blasted merchant's whereabouts. *Jem must be terrified,* she thought. He was, after all, only a child, unused to the dangers of . . .

Scarlet paused for a moment, then snapped her fingers and laughed out loud. A child in need of help. Right here on the islands. She couldn't have planned it better herself! It was exactly what her crew needed.

But now she was wasting precious seconds. She scanned the scene below her until she found the pirates and their prey and watched until she was fairly certain she knew which ship was theirs. Then she drew a breath and ran straight to the edge of the rooftop. She leaped across the gap to the next building, which she knew had a rain gutter, for she'd shimmied up and down it before during port raids. She put two fingers to her lips and let out one shrill blast, then another. The signal. Her crew would meet her at the ship, hopefully right away. There was no time to lose.

CHAPTER TWO

Jem Fitzgerald couldn't decide whether to stay calm or give in to the fear that swelled in his stomach. Sitting curled up on the floor of the cabin, chin resting on his knees, he watched the man pace before him and pondered his options. Master Davis from the King's Cross School for Boys would say, "Fear means you aren't being logical—a failing for any eleven-year-old boy." Master Davis had all the answers.

No fear then, Jem decided. He breathed in slowly, and the salty air that had seeped through the walls of the ship teased his nostrils.

Beside him, Uncle Finn grunted, "Quit staring, Jem," and shifted his egg-shaped body on the ship's creaking floorboards. "Or you'll be caught like that when they kill us both. Frozen for eternity with eyes like a giant flounder." He huffed and repositioned his weight like a restless hen.

The man before them stopped pacing and raised a furry eyebrow at Jem and his uncle. His fingers, yellow and thick as pipes, edged toward the cutlass that hung on his hip and hovered there a moment. Jem's eyes zeroed in on the man's middle finger—sliced off at the knuckle— then he forced himself to look at something else so he wouldn't be caught staring. Uncle Finn probably had a point. Jem had always been taught that it wasn't polite to stare, and he imagined this applied even to crusty-looking kidnappers. He dragged his gaze to the wall of the cabin, where a rat had evidently been at work, chewing a ragged hole in the baseboards. The man spat a neat gob near Jem's feet and continued pacing.

With a sigh, Uncle Finn closed his eyes and tapped his bald head against the wall behind him. Thin trails of sweat dripped down his cheeks and neck, pooling on the collar of his shirt. He hadn't stopped sweating since the moment they'd been pounced on in a Port Aberhard alley. Jem wanted to ask his uncle a hundred questions about this ship they'd been forced onto, the men who'd brought them here, and how best to untie the knots in the rope that bound their hands and ankles, but Uncle Finn had been losing patience with all his questions lately. So Jem followed his uncle's lead and closed his eyes to keep himself from staring.

He cracked one eye open a moment later, just to see if the scene before him had disappeared. It hadn't. Black boots crossed the floorboards with a firm, measured knock, pirouetted on one heel, then returned to the other side of the cabin. Jem opened both eyes and gazed up at the man's broad face, his angular teeth, and the wooden toothpick clamped between them. He wore a faded, gray shirt and a red head scarf that looked painfully tight. Jem's temples pulsed just looking at it. *Could this man be the real thing?* he wondered. He did a quick inventory. Tall black boots, check. Awful teeth, check. Severed knuckle—that got extra points. But could he really be a genuine, authentic—

"What're ye lookin' at?"

Jem hadn't noticed the man had come to a halt in front of him.

"Jem," Uncle Finn murmured, sounding exasperated. To himself, he added, "Serves me right, really. I should have known better than to bring—"

"Shut up, ye," their captor snarled. Uncle Finn's mouth formed a small O, then snapped shut.

"Haven't ye ever . . ." The man squatted before Jem and pressed his face so close that in the dim lamplight Jem could count the pores on his jaundiced skin. His breath smelled sour and vaguely familiar. Rotten eggs? Cream left to clot in the sun? "Haven't ye ever seen a pirate before?"

Jem stared into the dark tunnel between the man's front teeth, willed the jitters in his stomach to stop, and cocked his head to one side. "No," he said.

Of course he had never seen a pirate before. Nor had he, until two months ago, ever set foot on a ship that could cross one of the world's largest oceans. He'd never been in the presence of seamen with muscles like coiled rope or felt the toss of thirty-foot waves or the need to chuck overboard into roiling black water. So how could he know if he was, in fact, in the presence of a real buccaneer, a Jack-tar, a chantey-singing sea swab? Or if they even existed?

What would Master Davis think? Jem concentrated until he could hear his schoolmaster's voice: "Pirates? Nothing but a figment of the imagination, Jem. And we all know what imagination is: illogical."

"No," Jem repeated, transferring his stare from the man's teeth to his tarnished cutlass. "You're not really a pirate, are you?"

"Jem, for God's sake," Uncle Finn said. "Now would be an excellent time to stop asking questions." He turned to the man. "I'm sorry. Has to know everything, this one. Children these days. Question, question, question. It's all they do, really . . ." Uncle Finn's voice trailed off. The pirate shook his head, then rose and continued pacing.

Jem thought about defending himself and his right to find out exactly what was going on, but he decided now wasn't the time. Uncle Finn had no reason to get so irritated, though. He couldn't exactly tow his nephew across the ocean to find some peculiar treasure tucked away on one of four dozen tropical islands that lay scattered like puzzle pieces in a monstrous, blue bathtub and not expect a question or two, now could he?

Although, to be fair, Uncle Finn had explained a lot throughout their journey. Often, in fact, it had been hard to shut him up. Some nights he kept Jem awake studying maps and warning him of the dangers that awaited them in the tropics—stingrays, panthers, pirates with missing digits, even some disgruntled spirits that haunted the islands. Or so he said. More often, though, Uncle Finn kept him awake to memorize the Latin names of all the plants they'd encounter. Uncle Finn adored botany, but so far he hadn't been able to pass on the obsession to his nephew, who found the subject dead boring.

Still, Jem did owe his uncle some thanks, having convinced his parents to let him trade another year at the King's Cross School for Boys for a chance to explore the world. The decision had come as a surprise. A shock, really. He and Uncle Finn had never been particularly close. In fact, Jem barely knew the man, aside from what he'd learned when the great explorer descended on his family's house every few years to regale them with his tales from the tropics—the snakes he'd wrestled, the diseases he'd outwitted.

Jem hadn't even seen Uncle Finn in two years—not since his parents had enrolled him, despite his loudest protests and most exaggerated sighs, at the King's Cross School for Boys. He actually hadn't been home since. Not long after school began, Jem's father inherited an estate and moved his wife and their servants to another county, too far away for Jem to visit, even on holidays.

So when Uncle Finn turned up at the King's Cross to announce that he was whisking his nephew off on the adventure of a lifetime, Jem's wasn't the only jaw that dropped. Master Davis took one look at the aging explorer and shook his head in alarm. The somber schoolmaster had taken Jem under his wing from day one, when he confiscated Jem's favorite adventure novel ("*Lost in the Wild*? Stuff and nonsense, Jem.") and replaced it with his own beloved book ("*The Thinking Man's Guide to a Life Without Surprises*. Now there's a book!").

Master Davis had no imagination and a fierce, almost allergic aversion to adventure, but he meant well. He taught Jem that life at the King's Cross wasn't torturous, but "character-building," and that someday all the unpleasantness—being away from one's family, having one's favorite books seized—would make him a strong and practical man. "The end justifies the means" was one of Master Davis's favorite sayings, meaning the way in which a goal was achieved was less important than the actual achievement. Over the years Jem came to find his guidance sound and reassuring.

Uncle Finn, however, didn't see the schoolmaster's appeal. He waved off Master Davis's protests as if he were shooing away a fruit fly and produced a handwritten note from Jem's parents stating that they hoped the trip would inspire Jem to become a scientist himself. (This, Jem knew, was his mother's doing. The woman worshipped her brother Finn with such devotion that she'd row across the Atlantic herself if he suggested it.)

Uncle Finn had surveyed the drab, gray walls of the King's Cross courtyard and shuddered. "High time we got you out of this tomb, Jem. Not exactly conducive to learning, is it?"

"Don't worry, Master Davis," he called out to the schoolmaster, whose ears were burning a fierce shade of crimson, "I promise you that no sharks or boa constrictors will harm my nephew on his adventure. In six months time I'll return him back here, and he can continue to slowly die of boredom."

The notion that learning could take place far from a classroom suddenly filled Jem with hope and excitement, feelings that Master Davis squelched with a sharp frown. Immediately after Uncle Finn left to book their voyage, the schoolmaster began to advise Jem on how to build character while in the tropics.

"Keep your head about you, Jem," he'd say. "View everything with caution and healthy skepticism, and don't let yourself get caught up in all the"—he wrinkled his nose disdainfully—"excitement."

And so he continued right up until the day Jem left.

Jem was fairly certain Master Davis would faint if he knew how much excitement Jem had seen lately. After two months sailing across the Atlantic on the *Lady Eleanor*, they'd docked in Port Aberhard, the largest port town in the islands. There they'd found a boarding house where they'd hoped to spend a day or two readjusting to *terra firma*, as Uncle Finn called it, before hiring a boat to sail them to the island sketched on Uncle Finn's map. But they'd barely been on land for two hours when these so-called pirates descended on them as they left the tavern after dinner. It happened so quickly Jem still wondered if it were all a dream.

Light filled the cabin as the door swung open with a squeal, and a small, spectacled pirate sauntered in wearing an oversized blue coat that brushed his knees. He was followed by another man who was wrestling with Uncle Finn's massive, leather-bound trunk.

The small pirate walked, with strides far too long for someone his size, to the corner where Jem and Uncle Finn sat. He peered down at them over a thin, rodentlike nose and twitched his upper lip. His clothes were at least two sizes too big, but he looked determined to fill them, as if certain that, despite his age, he might still grow an inch. Or four. *Not exactly pirate material,* Jem thought.

"Finnaeus Bliss," the man said. He glanced quickly at

Jem, twitched his lip again, then focused on Uncle Finn. "I am, as I'm sure you know, the Dread Pirate Captain Wallace Hammerstein-Jones of the *Dark Ranger*." He paused, as if expecting fanfare or at least cries of recognition, but only an uncomfortable silence greeted him. Jem thought he saw the pacing pirate, who'd since stopped pacing, roll his eyes. But he couldn't be sure. The other man, tall with gargantuan shoulders, hummed a little tune to fill the void. The Dread Pirate Captain Wallace Hammerstein-Jones flared his nostrils at the man to silence him.

"It seems," the captain continued, "that you have some information we might find useful."

Uncle Finn said nothing, but he held the man's gaze.

"We've heard all about you, Bliss. You know these parts like an Islander. You know what lives and dies here. And I think you know where a certain treasure is hidden. Why else would you have returned?"

Uncle Finn stayed quiet, but the streams of sweat on his face now flowed like small rivers.

The Dread Pirate Captain Wallace Hammerstein-Jones crouched down, eyes wide and lip twitching uncontrollably. "Is it a map? Don't lie to me, Bliss. I know you have some tool to show you the way."

"I don't know what you're talking about, Captain," Uncle Finn said. Aside from the distinct waver in his uncle's voice, Jem thought him very brave. Like a hero in one of the adventure stories Jem used to read before Master Davis banned them. Except rounder. And with less hair. Yes, he decided, if Uncle Finn was willing to defy this man, then there was no reason to be scared.

The Dread Pirate, whose name Jem decided to shorten to Captain Wallace, pursed his lips and straightened to his full, unimposing height. "Fine. Oh, that's just fine. We'll find it ourselves." He snapped his fingers at the two men behind him. "The trunk."

"Right here," the man with the shoulders said, looking proud.

"Then open it," the captain said testily.

"But be careful!" Uncle Finn hastened to add. "There are breakables in there."

Captain Wallace smirked, but the massive man promised he'd be gentle.

"I'm Thomas, by the way," he added, waving a hand the size of a dinner plate.

"And I'm Iron Morgan," their first captor piped up, "but you can call me Pete." Iron "Pete" Morgan had suddenly dropped his pirate brogue and sounded much less bloodthirsty than he had a moment before. He squatted next to Jem and offered a calloused hand. "Sorry about my tone back then." He pointed to his head scarf. "Got a splitting headache." Now Jem knew there was nothing to fear. Real pirates wouldn't make pleasant conversation.

"What is this, a garden party?" Captain Wallace sneered. "Open that trunk."

Pete broke the locks, and Thomas began to pluck items out of the box. "A spyglass." He held the tube up to his eye.

"Lots of books." Pete fished out a stack.

"Other than the cap'n, Pete's the only pirate on board who can read," Thomas said, sounding like a proud parent. He peered over Pete's shoulder and asked, "What does that one say?"

"*A Natural History of Island Sym . . . Symbioses, Part One* by Finnaeus Bliss."

"That's ye." Thomas looked up at Uncle Finn. "Ye wrote a book?"

"Years ago, yes." Uncle Finn sounded pleased.

"That's right impressive—"

"On with it," Captain Wallace snapped.

"Underwear," Pete said into the trunk. "Sketching paper and pencils." He pulled his head out of the box. "You draw? So do I."

"He's good," Thomas added, fiddling with a homemade barometer. "'Specially his still lifes."

Captain Wallace rolled his eyes. Jem couldn't blame him. His crewmen were about as ferocious as oversized puppies.

The men searched through the entire trunk, leaving clothes, books, and mysterious handmade instruments strewn across the cabin. But they didn't find anything that would lead them to a treasure.

"Well, that's that," Thomas said. "Is it dinnertime? Ye two must be starved." Jem nodded, for he was far beyond hungry and had almost gotten used to the sickening void in his stomach. He guessed it had been a good five hours since they'd sat in the tavern and nearly inhaled what looked like flying fish but could have been anything with gills. After two months of hardtack and the occasional lime, Jem had welcomed anything that didn't taste like furniture.

"I'll get ye somethin' to eat," Thomas said and turned to go.

"Thomas, get back here," the captain ordered. Likely, Jem thought, Captain Wallace wanted to starve them until they gave in and spilled their secret.

But Pete interjected. "Captain, these men might be more willing to talk once they've had some food."

"You're too soft," the captain said. "But fine. Get them each a tack. When I return we'll"—he curled his twitching lip—"discuss." And he swept out of the cabin. Thomas followed behind, but Pete stayed to repack the trunk.

Jem looked at Uncle Finn, who'd turned a mottled shade of olive gray. "At least they're going to feed us," he said for conversation's sake, for he'd never known his uncle to be so quiet.

But Uncle Finn just shook his head. "It doesn't look good, Jem. The options are grim."

"But there's nothing to fear, right?" Jem said. He wriggled his wrists where the rope chafed. The knots felt loose and, with small hands like his, he might just . . .

"Nothing to fear? These are real pirates, boy. Plundering, pillaging pirates. They—" Uncle Finn stopped and watched Iron "Pete" Morgan neatly fold a pair of trousers.

"I don't know, I . . . hey! Uncle Finn." Jem lowered his voice to a whisper. He gestured with his head for

Uncle Finn to look at his hands, which had slipped free of their bonds.

Finally, a payoff for being undersized.

Uncle Finn glanced at Pete, who seemed absorbed in his task, then whispered, "Give me your hand."

Jem reached over to work on Uncle Finn's knots, but his uncle shook his head. "My sleeve," he mouthed without taking his eyes off Pete, now busy folding Uncle Finn's underwear.

Jem put his hand on the cuff of Uncle Finn's sleeve and felt, underneath the damp linen, the stiffness of paper. He'd gone and hidden it in his sleeve!

"Take it."

Alarmed, Jem began to protest. "I can't," he whispered. "I'll lose it for sure. Oh, you keep it. I—"

Uncle Finn's glare settled the matter. Jem slid the paper out of his uncle's sleeve and into his own just as Thomas returned with "dinner." He'd brought them each a lump of hardtack as dense as stone and probably less tasty. Jem slipped his hands back into their bonds just before Thomas offered to untie them.

"So ye can have a right proper dinner," Thomas said, looking pleased with himself.

"How kind," Uncle Finn muttered, and he took a bite of his tack. Or rather, he tried to bite it, but since it was practically petrified, he could only gnaw on it with his canines like a wolfhound on a bone.

"Thanks." Jem took his own meal and scraped his front teeth on one end of it. *More furniture,* he thought. *That figures.* "It's good."

Thomas knelt and watched them gnaw, looking concerned. "Just to warn ye," he said. "The Dread Pirate Cap'n Wallace . . . Hammer . . ." He broke off, having apparently forgotten the rest. "Ye know, the cap'n. He may not look like much, and between the two of ye, ye could prob'ly take him—"

"Shhh," Pete hissed, tilting his head toward the door.

"But he's got some temper," Thomas continued in a loud whisper. "If he wants somethin' bad enough, ye should save yerselves the fight and give it to him."

Uncle Finn sniffed.

"Oh, I'm sure ye want to find this treasure as badly as us, or anyone. Old King Aberhard did promise a fat reward, we all know that. But is it worth it to—"

The door squealed as it banged open again, and in walked the Dread Pirate Captain Wallace Hammerstein-Jones himself.

"*Bon appétit.*" The captain smirked and positioned himself in the center of the cabin, legs planted wide apart. The ship suddenly rolled over a wave, throwing him off balance for a moment. He righted himself quickly. "Tell me, Bliss. What do you know about this treasure?"

Uncle Finn set his dinner on his lap. "What do I know of this treasure . . . ," he said, and Jem noted with some relief that his uncle's voice no longer wavered. In fact, Jem felt a little sorry for the pirates. Anyone who knew Uncle Finn also knew to set aside at least an hour before requesting one of his stories. "I know that about seven years ago, one of Aberhard's men died of the mysterious Island Fever. Got a nasty cough, a deadly flu, then packed

24

it in." Uncle Finn straightened, getting into the story now. "It's a bacterial disease, you know, brought here to the islands by none other than the King's Men. Most, but not all of us, from the Old World are immune, but the Islanders, of course, were not.

"Now this man—Angus was his name, Admiral Angus—had spent years living with different groups of Islanders, and he knew the islands nearly as well as they, or so he said. When the Islanders began to show signs of the fever, he and many other King's Men hightailed it back to the Old World. But it was too late for Angus. He was one of the unlucky Old Worlders who wasn't immune.

"But on his deathbed, Angus began to speak of a treasure. He didn't actually come right out and describe it, but he did say . . ." And here Uncle Finn adopted the deep, theatrical voice Jem had heard so often when his uncle told his tales. *"On one of these fair islands lies a secret—a treasure, more valuable than anything we can harvest and ship home. He who finds it will fear nothing—no man nor spirit will touch him."*

Jem had heard Uncle Finn tell this story a dozen times. He could recite it himself, word for word. But this was the part that always drew Jem out of the story and sparked a million questions in his head. He could just hear Master Davis: "Spirits? Ha. Nothing but children's stories."

Although Jem used to enjoy reading stories about magic and ghosts, after two years under Master Davis's instruction, he had to agree with his teacher. In all his eleven years, he'd never seen a ghost.

"Angus insisted that since he'd followed the Islanders right to the treasure, they'd known about it all along, and they felt safe in its presence," Uncle Finn continued. "Of course, by that time the island people were well on their way to extinction, and the fever had entered Angus's brain. He passed on soon after, taking the rest of the details with him. The king was rather put out by his admiral dropping off at such an inconvenient time, but the treasure boosted his spirits. Without knowing whether it was a heap of jewels or a potion to ward off restless spirits, King Aberhard proclaimed that whoever found this treasure, be it a pirate or servant of the crown, would be richly rewarded."

The pirates looked dazed long after Uncle Finn stopped talking.

"Right. Well." Captain Wallace snapped out of it first. "We know all that. Obviously we wouldn't be here if we didn't. You avoided the question nicely. Now tell me, Bliss, what *you* know about this treasure. What is it? Where is it hidden?"

Uncle Finn gave him a long, solemn look. "I know nothing more."

"Nothing? Oh, don't be so modest, Bliss. I heard from a reliable source that you have a map showing the way to the treasure."

"I have no such map," Uncle Finn said, looking the captain directly in the eye.

True, Jem thought, fingering the paper in his sleeve. *That's true.*

Captain Wallace pivoted on one boot heel, stalked

to the wall, then returned. His lip twitched, steady as a pulse. One eyebrow arched above his spectacles like a bow poised to release an arrow.

"Don't tease me, Bliss. You have no idea what I'm capable of. I'm asking you to join us, share your information, then share the treasure and the reward. Your life depends on your next answer, and I'll only ask you once more."

"Tell him," Thomas mouthed.

"Where is the map?"

Jem looked at Pete, who returned a calm, level gaze. He knew there was nothing to worry about. Uncle Finn would just give a simple answer, then they'd be on their way, back to the boarding house, to bed, and—

"No." Uncle Finn's voice was firm. "You will not know."

Captain Wallace's ashen face turned fuchsia in a second. "P-p-p," he sputtered, trying to regain control of his twitching lip. "P-p-plank!"

"Captain, no." Pete gasped and stepped between the captain and Uncle Finn.

"PLANK!" the captain screamed and hurled himself out the cabin door. "Now!" His cry carried down the hall.

"What does he mean?" Jem cried, looking at his uncle desperately. "He doesn't . . . they don't really do that. Only in stories. That's nonsense, right? It's a bluff."

Then, all at once, the room was full of pirates shouting and shoving as if they'd materialized right out of the walls. Two seized Uncle Finn's arms and one grabbed his legs. His uneaten dinner clattered to the floor. "Leave the boy. Let him go!" Uncle Finn hollered as the pirates dragged him, struggling, out the cabin door.

"Uncle Finn!" Jem tried to stand and follow, but Pete pulled him back and threw a heavy arm over him. "What are they doing? They're not really—"

Pete clamped his hands over Jem's ears and stared at the wall.

But Jem heard it, anyway, muffled through Pete's fingers. The hollers in the hall, boots stomping up to the deck and across to the stern. A pause, then . . . *splash*.

CHAPTER THREE

"Let me go!" Jem hollered into Pete's arm, squirming like an eel pinned beneath it. He struggled to his feet, forgetting they were bound, then tripped and toppled over onto the pirate. Jem lay still for a moment, gasping, cheek pressed against the damp floorboards. This couldn't be happening. They couldn't have made Uncle Finn walk the plank. That splash he'd heard—it must have been something else. A fish jumping, maybe. A really big one.

"Where is he? What have you done with him?" Jem shouted at Pete, who promptly moved over and sat on top of him, square in the middle of Jem's back, pinning him to the floor.

"It looks bad, doesn't it?" Pete said. He bowed his head and interlaced his yellowed fingers in his lap like a child awaiting punishment in the headmaster's office. "I bet you think we're monsters, don't you? But try to see it from a pirate's point of view. We're not that bad, really. We share. We commiserate. And all those deadly sins . . . gluttony, sloth, using the captain's name in vain . . . we don't do that. Well, all right, sometimes we do, but only when . . ."

Jem stopped listening and searched for words to fill his open mouth.

Thomas poked his great head through the door like

an anxious Saint Bernard. "He all right?" he asked Pete, nodding toward Jem, who finally found a few words to spew.

"All right?" Jem twisted to look back at Pete, aware that his voice was shrill and panicked. "All right? You killed . . ." And he sank back to the floor, unable to complete the sentence. "You—you didn't really, did you?"

"Um . . ." Thomas tugged nervously on a lock of his hair.

Pete pierced him with a glare. "Yes. Yes, we did, Thomas. The boy's right. His uncle's dead." He stood up.

"But—" Thomas began.

"Stop it."

"You stop."

"Both of you stop!" Jem cried, scrambling to his knees. "What's going on? Did you or didn't you make him walk the plank?"

The pirates exchanged glares, then Thomas bowed his head and kicked at the floorboards.

"Look here, boy," Pete said, lifting Jem up by his small shoulders and leaning him against the wall like a rag doll. "You've got to understand the pirate life. We do what we must to get by. It's a dangerous place, the tropics—with its cursed beasts and crazy squalls. And then there's your old king and his men, traipsing around like they own the place, pillaging and plundering more than all of us pirates put together. Except they're stealing from the land and the people, or what's left of them. Thought they'd just take a jaunt across the drink and nip up a few unclaimed islands. Well, we pirates like to throw a few obstacles in their way. It's right honorable of us, really."

Thomas nodded. "He's right. Being a pirate ain't so bad. It's a way of life. Like bein' a . . . a blacksmith. Or a priest. Ye do what you must. Ye'll see."

"What do you mean, I'll see?" Jem didn't like the sound of that.

Just then the door swung open and in walked Captain Wallace, looking slightly more disheveled than he had when he left. His blue coat hung off one shoulder and his spectacles sat crooked on his small snout. The captain looked from Thomas to Pete, then settled his gaze on Jem.

"Well now. That's done." He pushed the bridge of his spectacles up his nose with his index finger and straightened his coat. He cleared his throat. "Yes. Well. Let that be a lesson to you." The three pirates exchanged a glance, then Thomas shrugged and shuffled out of the cabin. On his way out he patted Jem's head.

Jem ducked out of his reach. He squeezed his eyes shut and replayed the events of the last few minutes: the pirates bursting into the room and seizing Uncle Finn, the splash he'd heard even through Pete's rough hands. His uncle was gone. Floundering out there in the dark waves . . .

Jem shook his head and fought the panic rising in his chest. He couldn't think about that. Not now. The man before him was dangerous, and Jem was at his mercy.

"And so, boy," Captain Wallace began, "it comes down to you. You now know what happens to men who defy me. You wouldn't want that to happen to you." He gestured toward the door through which Uncle Finn had disappeared. "But you wouldn't let it, would you?" The captain's eyes narrowed as he stepped closer to Jem. "You're smarter than the old man. Who is he to you, anyway? Not your father?"

Jem bit his lip and tried to push thoughts of Uncle Finn out of his mind so he could think logically. Offering a pirate one's personal information didn't seem logical. But then again, neither did getting oneself killed by that pirate. How he wished he were back in the Old World, maybe on a courtyard stroll with Master Davis. Or a visit home from school, if his parents would allow it. His mother's maid would be flitting around him, insisting he drink his broth or else he'd never grow tall and his boots would always be two sizes too big because—

"Answer!" Captain Wallace cried.

"Uncle," Jem blurted out without thinking. "He is . . . he was . . . my uncle."

"Your uncle," Captain Wallace repeated in a singsong voice. "My condolences then. But now, here's your chance to right your uncle's wrongs. The old fool refused to share his information." He *tsk*ed. "Rather selfish, don't you agree? But you, nephew of Finnaeus Bliss, I'm going to give you a chance to make the right decision."

Jem shook his head. He'd stopped listening after "old fool." His uncle did tend to go on at length about orchids and ferns and especially bromeliads, but he was no fool. "I don't—"

"Wrong answer!" Captain Wallace bellowed like

a foghorn. He bent forward, grasped Jem's collar, and lifted him a good foot off the ground. "Don't be stupid, boy. You've seen what pirates do to stupid people." He shot small bullets of spit onto Jem's face with every *s*.

"Um, Captain." Pete cleared his throat.

"What?" Captain Wallace, still clutching Jem's collar, cast him an irritated glance. Pete motioned for him to release the boy, and the captain let out a great sigh before dropping Jem back on the floor. Pete tugged the captain over to a corner where they conversed in mime—Jem caught the gestures for throat-slitting, beheading with a broadsword, and what looked like being eaten alive by wild bunnies. The pirates paused their pantomime twice to study Jem. Then Pete returned and knelt beside him.

"Look, boy. You don't have much choice here. Either you tell the captain what he wants to know or you get killed. No compromises, I'm afraid. Come on, now. Tell him, and he'll keep you around. There're worse things than being a pirate. We'll win no beauty contests, sure, but you'll never want for fresh air."

The absurdity of the situation, the complete lack of logic, suddenly struck Jem like a tidal wave. A mere two months ago he'd been living at the King's Cross School for Boys, getting trampled on the football field, envying the care packages his dorm mates received from home. And now here he was, captive on a pirate ship, risking death if he didn't join them.

He couldn't help it.

He laughed.

Captain Wallace started. "What? Why's he laughing?"

"Shut up, boy," Pete hissed. "Just say yes."

"You know how I get when people laugh at me. Why's he laughing?" Captain Wallace's voice rose half an octave.

Jem shrugged and tried unsuccessfully to smother his panicked giggles.

"That's it." Captain Wallace stamped his boot on the floorboards. "Take him to the—"

"Cap'n!" A wail echoed in the hall, followed by a thunder of boot steps. Jem heard the *shing* of cutlasses being unsheathed and a chorus of oaths. Then Thomas shoved his great head through the doorway again. His eyes had grown to twice their size.

"We're being attacked!" he cried, then galloped off down the hall.

"Attacked?" Captain Wallace gave Pete an irritated look. "We can't be under attack. Who'd attack us?"

Pete shrugged and ducked out the door, hand on his cutlass. The captain and Jem were left staring at each other while boot steps and hollers reverberated above them. Captain Wallace opened his mouth as if to speak, then shut it.

Moments later, Pete dove back into the cabin, a pale glow in his yellow cheeks. "Captain," he gasped. "We've got a problem."

"What? Who? It's not that cursed Blackjack again, is it? I already cut off his hands and three of his most important toes. What more does he want?"

"Not Blackjack, Captain." Pete's eyes searched the room as if he were looking for a place to hide.

"Then who?" the captain howled.

"It's the . . ." Pete shrugged helplessly. "The Ship of Lost Souls."

"No." Captain Wallace shrank back into his oversized coat.

"The which?" Jem had to ask.

"Oh God! Hide! No, scratch that! Attack!" Captain Wallace gripped his broadsword. "If we're going to die at the hands of the Lost Souls, we're going to die fighting! Go on now. I'll be in my room." He scurried out of the cabin. Pete looked down at Jem as if he'd suddenly remembered the boy existed.

"Um . . . stay here," he ordered, and disappeared out the door.

"Stay here," Jem repeated, obeying the order for the moment. He exhaled slowly and took stock of his situation. As far as he could see, he had two options: sit tight until the pirates returned or these so-called Lost Souls happened upon him, or try to escape.

It wasn't a difficult decision. Jem tossed aside the rope that had bound his hands and began to work on the knots around his ankles.

It felt good to stand up again, although his knees wobbled a little. He paused for a moment, listening to the clamor above him. It sounded frantic, as if no one could decide which way to run. The Ship of Lost Souls, Pete had said. It had an ominous ring to it. But, Jem reasoned, it might give him the chance he needed to escape. Or at least hide somewhere until he could escape. He'd take a ship of Lost Souls over a ship of angry pirates any day.

He was, after all, something of a lost soul himself.

"Be brave. Keep your head," he muttered to himself as he slipped out into the hallway. Although he and Uncle Finn had been blindfolded when the pirates had dragged them on board the *Dark Ranger*, Jem figured he'd be able to find his way around the ship without much trouble. One ship must be like any other, and this one, so far, looked much like the *Lady Eleanor*. He was now on the level below the main deck where the pirates slept and maybe even hid their plunder. At the far end of the hall stood a staircase, and Jem crept up it, following the noises of battle and the pungent smell of the sea.

He climbed toward a banner of stars speckled over an indigo sky. Soon the cool night breeze greeted his face, and he found himself standing on the main deck, under the towering foremast. As he'd thought, the layout of the *Dark Ranger* was very similar to that of the *Lady Eleanor*: It was double-masted with a gun deck, a quarterdeck, a small poop deck at the back of the vessel, and a forecastle deck—which sailors called the fo'c'sle—at the front. He took comfort in that familiarity. Indeed, if he closed his eyes and concentrated on the sway from the waves rolling under him, he could almost believe he was back on the *Lady Eleanor*, still en route to the tropics in search of the mysterious treasure. Uncle Finn would be standing beside him, knotting a rope to test their sailing speed and telling unbelievable tales from the tropics, like the one about the rubies that fell from the sky. Yes, it was all a lark again, nothing to fear—not with his uncle beside him . . .

Two pirates clumped by, cursing, and pulled Jem out of his dream. He dove back down the staircase into the shadows. He needed to find a good hiding place where he could watch the action and contemplate his next move.

On the *Lady Eleanor* there had been a trapdoor under the foremast, under which Jem had hidden a few times to escape Uncle Finn's lectures on bromeliads. He now scanned the *Dark Ranger*'s deck for a similar compartment and couldn't believe his luck: an iron handle gleamed on the floorboards nearby. Jem launched himself toward it, yanked up on the handle, and dove inside without a thought to who or what might already be occupying the space.

Thankfully, it seemed empty, although the darkness was so deep that it was hard to tell, and Jem had learned that dark spaces on ships tended to be inhabited by rats. He shuddered and pushed the door open above him just enough to peer out. A pirate with a red sash tied around his waist ran by, shouting something about devilish ghouls to no one in particular. Then Jem saw an odd sight: a small figure in a hooded black cloak. At least, that's what he thought he saw, but it darted by so quickly he couldn't be sure. But wait—there was another, no taller than himself and scurrying faster than a cockroach. What on earth?

Just then the door above him swung wide open and a massive figure started squeezing itself into his space, feetfirst and grunting. Panicked, Jem pressed himself against the wall. His hiding space could hold perhaps three of him, four at the most. He'd never go unnoticed, especially not with his heart thumping like the drum major in the King's Cross marching band. Boot heels hit the floor, and a hairy arm brushed against his face.

"Who's there?" a familiar voice gasped. "Oh God, ye ain't one of them, are ye?"

"*Shh*. Thomas, it's me," Jem whispered. Thomas, he was fairly certain, would do him no harm. His heartbeats quieted down.

"Boy!" Thomas said, sounding relieved. "Ye're a smart one to hide. If ye go back out there ye'll soon feed the fish."

"Who are they?" Jem asked, hoping to distract the giant from the obvious fact that he'd escaped the cabin below deck. "The Ship of Lost Souls. What is it?"

"Shivers, boy, ye don't know? A seaman's worst nightmare, that's what." Thomas's voice trembled in the dark. "'Bout ten years ago, a wee ship called the *Margaret's Hope* set sail from a port school with a few schoolmasters and sons of the King's Men on board, out on some expedition. Studyin' geography or somethin'. Got caught in a hurricane, they did. Never seen again."

A torrent of footsteps rattled over the trapdoor, and Jem ducked instinctively. The sound of the footsteps faded, and Thomas continued. "But not long after, sailors began to talk of a strange sight: a small ship, like the *Margaret's Hope*, glidin' like a ghost over the sea. And ghostly she was. Manned by spirits of the dead, they say. The Lost Souls haunt the waters, cloaked and hooded, and if they catch yer vessel, well, God help ye."

"Ghosts?" Jem repeated. "The *Dark Ranger* has been invaded by ghosts?" He shook his head. It just got more and more absurd. No one back home would believe a speck of it.

"Ye haven't been here long, have ye, boy? Ye'll see. These islands are full of spirits. And not kindly ones, either." Jem heard him search around in the darkness for the latch, then push the door open a crack.

"Look," Thomas said, and they both peered out. Four pirates thundered by, yelling and stumbling over one another. Behind them, two cloaked figures darted and pranced like little demons. Jem swore he could hear mischievous laughter.

"Good Lord," he said, half to himself. "Where . . . where am I?"

"Told you, boy, it's a crazy place. The islands are full of spirits and magic. Bad magic." Jem felt Thomas shiver beside him, and he trembled, too, despite the logical side of his brain that was still scoffing at the notion of ghosts and magic. "But now, I can't stay and chat. Cap'n told me to hide all the pieces of eight we got down below. Just raided a man-o'-war last week, we did. And—" Thomas stopped and clapped his great hand to his mouth. "Whoops. Forget I said that. My big yap, it gets me into all sorts of trouble. But ye won't tell, will you? Ye're pretty well one of us now."

With that, Thomas hauled his giant frame out of their hiding space. He paused before closing the trapdoor. "Stay here until I come back for you." And then he was gone.

"Stay here," Jem repeated for the second time that night. "Not likely." For Thomas had just reminded him of the greatest danger he faced, far worse than whatever fiends were prancing about the ship. Jem was now expected to join the *Dark Ranger* pirates, prisoner on the dark seas, so far from home, and without his uncle. He had to escape. He had to get home. But for once, he couldn't think of anything resembling a logical plan.

He opened the trapdoor and clambered back into the cool night air. Shouts and shuffles drifted over from the poop deck, near the stern. Jem crept in the opposite direction to the fo'c'sle and peered over at the waves. Swimming was out; he could only dog-paddle, and there was no land in sight. Maybe he could find another good spot to hide until they docked in some port. But who knew when that might be? And where would he hide? The pirates would scour the schooner as soon as they realized he was missing.

Then he saw a small ship, perhaps one-third the size of the *Dark Ranger*, rocking against its starboard side and tied to the pirates' ship by a thick rope and a grappling iron. It had a single mast but looked sturdy. At first Jem assumed it belonged to the pirates who used it perhaps for sneak attacks on other ships. But then a beam of moonlight illuminated a name scrawled in chipped white paint on its side. *Margaret's Hop*. The final *e* must have eroded over the years thanks to the salty waves. It was the Ship of Lost Souls. Somehow Jem had pictured it veiled in eerie mist. But the Ship of Lost Souls was just a normal ship—although tiny and in need of a good cleaning.

A scuffle behind him made Jem turn. Three Lost Souls had surrounded Captain Wallace, pressing him against the mainmast. They were playing "monkey in the middle" with the captain's spectacles, dancing in circles around him.

"Stop it. Leave me alone," Captain Wallace whined, squinting at the ghouls who mimicked him with glee.

"Boy!" Thomas came running across the deck, straight for Jem. "I told ye to stay put. Get back down below!" His shouts drew the captain's attention, and Captain Wallace squinted in Jem's direction.

"The boy? Bliss's nephew?" For a moment he ignored the devils pirouetting around him. "Grab him, Thomas! Tie him back up!"

Jem ducked out of Thomas's reach and took off running toward the stern. Now he was in for it. There was nowhere to hide out here. Those churning waves were looking rather inviting.

Just then, two big hands seized Jem's shoulders and stopped him in his tracks. To his surprise, they weren't Thomas's arms pulling him back, but arms cloaked in black. The arms of a Lost Soul! Jem yelped and tried to wrench himself free, but the thing held fast.

"Stop struggling." It spoke! Jem tried to shove it away, but the Lost Soul was much stronger than he was. It threw a long arm around his waist and pulled him toward the grappling iron that attached the *Margaret's Hop* to the *Dark Ranger*. The other two spirits joined them, and four more appeared out of the shadows. Together they backed away from the pirates, who watched, helpless, as more and more Lost Souls emerged—a swarm of black hoods. Thomas looked like he might cry. Silently, one by one, the figures launched themselves off the side of the ship and rappelled down the rope to the sloop below. Jem couldn't believe it—he was being kidnapped from his kidnappers!

"Our turn," Jem's new captor said in a low, grumbly voice, nudging him toward the edge. "Hold the rope tight and let yourself down." When Jem hesitated, the thing gave him a shove.

"What would Master Davis do in my place?" Jem wondered aloud as he dangled his legs over the dark Atlantic and the ship of cloaked ghouls. Chalk it all up to building character? Try to reason with the Lost Souls?

"Please let me wake up to discover it's all been a dream," Jem said. Then he shut his eyes, imagined himself back at school, and slid down the rope. Oh sure, the King's Cross wasn't the most thrilling place to live. But at least at school he was safe. Suddenly the predictability of a life completely without surprises seemed downright appealing.

Jem opened his eyes when his feet connected with the deck of the *Margaret's Hop*. He sighed. If this was a dream, it wasn't over yet.

His captor dropped onto the deck behind him, then used a dagger to cut the rope that tied them to the pirate ship. "All hands on deck!" it hollered, as the sloop began to drift away from the *Dark Ranger*. Jem looked up at the ship he'd just escaped from. Thomas leaned over the side, waving a handkerchief like a forlorn mother. Beside him stood the Dread Pirate Captain Wallace Hammerstein-Jones, tearing at his hair and crying, "You let him get away! The treasure was about to be ours, and you let him get away!" His voice faded into the night.

For a few minutes the Lost Souls seemed to forget about Jem, abandoning him on the deck while they ran about the ship, calling orders like "All hands!" and "Weigh anchor!"

The Lost Soul who was manning the wheel chose a course, and off they sailed into the darkness, away from Captain Wallace's wails. And away from Uncle Finn, wherever he was.

Jem gave into his wobbly knees and sank down to the floorboards, which smelled vaguely rotten and moldy. He tried to swallow the lump in his throat as he remembered the times he'd tuned out Uncle Finn's lectures on flowering shrubs. Or faked sick to be excused. How could he have been so thoughtless? But he didn't get far into the memory, for soon the Lost Souls returned and formed a huddle around him, their dark cloaks rustling.

A few of the ghouls chuckled, and Jem dared to look up at them, expecting the worst. What could come next on this disastrous adventure? A fateful plank walking? Or something more torturous? But the ghouls made no move to hurt him, until the biggest one—his captor, Jem was certain—poked him in the ribs with the toe of its boot.

"Leave him alone," another Lost Soul spoke up. "He's scared."

"Yeah, Lucas. Don't touch him."

A demon named Lucas? Absurd. But Jem had come to expect as much. He'd just lie still and hope the dream would end soon.

"But look what I found on him earlier," the one named Lucas said. "Looks like a map."

Uncle Finn's map! Jem's head shot up, and he struggled to his knees. He hadn't even noticed it missing from his sleeve.

"Give it here." Another ghoul snatched it from Jem's captor.

"No!" Jem shouted. They would not have his map, his uncle's pride, and his last bit of Uncle Finn. Without thinking logically—for by now he was far beyond thinking logically—Jem threw himself at the Lost Soul who was holding his map and tackled it to the floor. "Give it back!"

The ghoul fell with a shriek, although not the shriek one would expect from the dead. A softer, more human shriek. Jem pinned it to the floor, his knee on its chest, and grabbed the map. Another Lost Soul lunged at him from the side, but he elbowed it. Then—for now he had nothing to lose—he grasped the ghost's hood and yanked it back.

The ghoul had hair. And large, dark eyes. And a mouth, wide open. Jem froze as his unbelievable adventure reached new heights of illogicality.

The Lost Soul was a girl. A dark-haired, dark-eyed, very angry girl.

CHAPTER FOUR

Although Scarlet McCray spent a good portion of her time in disguise, not once had anyone ever uncloaked her. For a moment she could only stare, openmouthed, at the boy who crouched over her, his bony knee jabbing into her chest. With one swift kick and a twist, she could have him pinned to the mast with her dagger to his Adam's apple.

But as she reached for her weapon, hidden deep inside her cloak, she saw the fear in his eyes. First kidnapped by pirates, then by a bunch of cloaked ghouls—could she blame him for reacting the way he had? So, instead of knocking him overboard and leaving him for shark bait, she nodded at his knee.

"Get off me."

The boy scuttled backward, crablike, still staring at her. "I'm sorry," he said. "I didn't . . . you're a . . ."

"Girl. Yes. Observant." Scarlet rolled her eyes, used to this routine. Blah blah unladylike, blah blah petticoats. Blah. She hopped up and offered the boy a hand. He eyed it the way she herself might eye a plate of slimy oysters and scrambled to his feet without her help. Then he glanced around at her crew members, who surrounded them, still cloaked.

"So if you're a girl, then none of you are really . . ."

"Come on, mates," Scarlet said. "Off with the hoods.

Stop confusing him." She turned back to the boy. "What's your name?" Of course, she already knew, but telling him that would likely scare him even more. She wondered what had happened to his uncle Finn and why she hadn't been able to find the man during her quick search of the *Dark Ranger*.

"Jem. Jem Fitzgerald." He watched incredulously as Scarlet's crew members began to peel off their hoods, revealing a motley gang of children with identical mischievous grins.

Scarlet turned to look at her crew. There were twenty-three Lost Souls in total: small ones and gangly ones, pale ones and dark ones, dirty ones and—well, they were all in need of a good bath. There were Lost Souls with loose teeth and Lost Souls with lisps and even a few who could turn backflips across the deck. She surveyed them all and nodded, satisfied.

One about Jem's size stepped forward. "Timothy Sanders," he said and presented his hand. "Quartermaster and resident nautical genius."

"But you can call him Drivelswigger," a taller one with sand-colored hair piped up, shrugging off his heavy cloak. "Or Swig for short. That one spends far too much time with his head in the books." The boy welcomed Jem with a wide grin and a wink. "I'm Smitty, but you can call me Hurricane Smith."

"If you can say it with a straight face." Scarlet gave the boy a friendly nudge. "None of us can. He's just Smitty."

A freckled, ginger-haired brother and sister duo shed

their cloaks and slipped forward to introduce themselves. Liam and Ronagh Flannigan. Jem looked surprised at the sight of another pirate girl—a reaction that Scarlet had seen countless times among new recruits. Especially those fresh off a boat from the Old World. And Jem Fitzgerald, as Scarlet knew from earlier observation, could be the spokes-boy for the Old World.

One by one, the Lost Souls uncloaked and introduced themselves, until only two of Scarlet's crew members remained hidden under their hoods. Lucas Lawrence and Gil Jenkins, of course. But before Scarlet had to repeat the order, Lucas pulled off his hood to reveal a blockish head and limbs that looked like they belonged on an adult rather than a thirteen-year-old boy. Lucas's skin stretched tight over his bones, as if trying desperately to stop them from growing even more. He stuck out a large hand, calloused from carpentry chores, and muttered his name. Gil Jenkins followed suit, always imitating his much larger companion's manners. In Scarlet's opinion, Lucas Lawrence was the last person on earth anyone ought to imitate, but she kept those thoughts to herself. Most of the time.

"So you're a ship of . . . children?" Jem asked once the introductions were over. He still looked like he'd been walloped in the gut.

"Speak for yourself, lad." Smitty stuck out his chest with pride. "I just turned thirteen."

"We're all between thirteen"—Scarlet gestured to Smitty, Lucas, and a few of the other boys—"and eight." She nodded at little Ronagh, who wrinkled her nose.

"I'm twelve," Scarlet added. She didn't have to look at Lucas to know he was sneering.

Jem looked at her but avoided her eyes. "I didn't get your name," he told her chin.

"Oh. Well, I'm Captain McCray. But everyone calls me Scarlet." Once again she stretched out her hand, and once again Jem only stared.

"You're the captain?" he said.

Smitty clapped a hand on Jem's shoulder. "You'll get used to it, Jem. This one's no damsel in distress. Don't even think about holding a door open for her." Scarlet swatted him upside the head. "Now, mates," Smitty continued, "we've got a jolly bounty, which those pirates so kindly donated to our cause. And we've got a new crew member. I'd say it's time for a midnight celebration."

The Lost Souls cheered and broke from their huddle to scatter every which way across the deck.

"Someone check the sails first!" Scarlet hollered after them. Then she turned to Jem, ready to offer him a dry spot on the floor in one of the cabins. *He must be exhausted, being kidnapped and rescued all in a day,* she thought. But Jem had suddenly turned a sickly shade of green, and it occurred to Scarlet that they might have consulted him before making the "new crew member" announcement.

The sound of Liam Flannigan's pipe flute and Smitty's off-key warble twirled on an easterly wind that teased the sails of the *Margaret's Hop*. Ronagh Flannigan and the younger pirates sat cross-legged on the deck with a small feast in front of them, including dried herring smothered in strawberry preserves—both stolen from the pirates. Tim and a pair of pale twins named Emmett and Edwin stood nearby, examining the spectacles they'd lifted off the whiny little captain with the impossibly long name. Tim clapped his hands in time with Liam's tune as the ship's unofficial musician hopped around, flute to his lips. Smitty followed Liam's steps, singing tunelessly over mouthfuls of fresh oyster, also pinched during that evening's raid and despised by everyone else on board. "Ain't it plunderful to be a pirate?" Smitty sang.

Scarlet looked down on the fun from the fo'c'sle, where she'd stationed herself to scan the dark waters for unexpected obstacles like islands or other ships. But only miles of blackest night stretched before her. She smiled at the sight of her crew in a celebratory mood. Her plan had worked: They'd fulfilled their mission by helping a child in need. Below her, Smitty launched into his favorite sea chantey in his best crusty pirate voice.

> *I'm not your average buccaneer,*
> *A bully on the waters.*
> *I'm still too young to grow a beard—*
> *No need to hide your daughters.*
> *(Yet.)*
>
> *A jolly life we lead upon*
> *The fair and sparkling sea.*

I won't go back; forevermore
A pirate I will be.

Mine ain't your typ'cal childhood.
I bet you'd be astonished.
I wield a cutlass and a knife
And never get admonished.
   (Well, sometimes.)

A jolly life we lead upon
The fair and sparkling sea.
I won't go back; forevermore
A pirate I will be.

See, here upon the Margaret's Hop,
No grown-ups are allowed.
No one to tell us when to stop
or when we're being too loud.
   (Except Tim, when he snores.
   Yes, you do, Swig. I have to listen to it.)

A jolly life we lead upon
The fair and sparkling sea.
I won't go back; forevermore
A pirate I will be.

Although everyone had heard the song before, they
all laughed—even Lucas Lawrence, who rarely joined

in on anything that didn't involve raiding other pirate ships and counting pillaged pieces of eight. Scarlet had to admit, however, that even though Lucas had the social skills of a giant squid, he did valuable work on board, like repairing the *Hop*'s hull and mast. Lucas had apprenticed as a carpenter's assistant for a year before joining the Lost Souls and was almost as useful on board as a real grown-up. Well, as useful as grown-ups could be.

One person, however, didn't join in the merriment. Jem Fitzgerald sat on a barrel off to the side of the mainmast, chin on his fist, lips clamped in a tight line. Scarlet watched him for a moment, then resolved to draw him out of his gloom. As captain, it was her job to make everyone on board feel at home. She called for another Lost Soul to take her place on the fo'c'sle and skipped down to the main deck, glad to be out of her Lost Soul disguise and feeling like herself again in a shirt and trousers, without a cap to hide her hair.

Jem was staring out at the black sea, not even paying attention to Smitty's antics and Liam's jigging feet. Scarlet sidled up to him and hopped up onto the barrel beside his. She swung her legs in time to the music and looked straight at the boy until he could no longer ignore her. He muttered an uncomfortable hello.

"Smitty's a bit of a nut." Scarlet nodded toward the light-footed boy pirate, who was now searching for a word to rhyme with "landlubber." Jem didn't respond, so Scarlet pressed on. "No one knows his real name, see. 'Smitty' comes from 'Smith,' his last name. It's like you calling yourself . . . oh, I don't know, 'Fitz,' short for Fitzgerald. Hey, that's not a bad name, is it? Fitz. I like it." Scarlet was fond of nicknames.

"Anyway," she continued, "from the first day he joined the crew, about a year ago, Smitty refused to tell anyone his first name. 'Parently it's a painful one. That's why you'll hear us sometimes call out 'Horace' or 'Ignatius,' just to see if he answers."

Jem nodded, glanced at Smitty, and returned his gaze to the water. Scarlet, who ranked awkward silences nearly as high as raw oysters on her list of Most Despised, pressed on again.

"Smitty comes from a rich family that owns a plantation on one of the islands. Sugarcane, I think. Or tobacco. Anyway, he saw us clowning around and stealing supplies in port last year, thought we looked like better companions than his boring old parents, and followed us back to the *Hop*. Then he threatened to rat us out to everyone we'd stolen from unless we took him with us. Came on board that very day, Smitty did. He's a lark."

Jem's eyes flitted from the ocean to Scarlet and back to the ocean. "He left his family?"

"He did," she answered, happy to have finally enticed the boy to speak. She added, "And who wouldn't?" at the same time as Jem asked, "But why?"

"Why?" Scarlet repeated. "I just told you why. We looked like better companions."

"I know," Jem interrupted. "But how could he just leave his parents?"

"How could he not?" Scarlet said. "Fitz, we're a ship full of pirate children! We sail the seas without grown-ups to disappoint us or tell us what to do." She waved at the party going on beside them. "I mean, how often does this happen where you're from? Admit it, it's far past your bedtime, right?"

Jem seemed to consider this for a moment, then conceded. Encouraged, Scarlet drove her point home. "And think of it: We practically rule these waters. You saw those pirates' faces when we hopped on board to save you. How jolly was that?"

Jem started. "You came to save me?"

Scarlet shrugged, wanting to act modest even though she knew it'd been a brilliant capture. "I saw you and your uncle get kidnapped in Port Aberhard," she said, omitting the part about spying on them. And the fact that her motivation hadn't been entirely selfless. She had needed this raid to inspire the crew as much as Jem needed a rescue. "Anyway, it was a fun raid. Who wouldn't want to join our crew?"

Jem settled his chin on his fist again and sighed. "I think I'd rather go home." Then he added, "But only if the last day had never happened."

Although a little taken aback—he was the first recruit ever to show any reluctance to join the Lost Souls—Scarlet was intrigued by Jem's ominous tone and the look of longing in his eyes. She gave him a friendly nudge with her elbow. "What's your story, Fitz?"

Jem clicked his tongue against his teeth and took a breath. At first his story trickled out slowly, but as he gathered speed and confidence, it began to gush like a river approaching the sea: a voyage across the Atlantic with a near-famous uncle, an abduction by pirates, a refusal to comply with the pirates resulting in the near-famous uncle being forced to walk the plank.

Scarlet nearly tipped her barrel, leaning so far forward to hear the tale. Now she understood the boy's distress and even his reluctance to join their merry crew. He seemed like a good sort, this Jem, despite his pish-posh accent. He'd make a fine young pirate once he got his hands a little dirty, of that she was certain. But if she didn't play this right, he would be the first child she'd ever met who genuinely didn't want to join her crew. And that would positively scuttle.

When Jem's tale came to an end, Scarlet felt a fierce urge to help him. The Ship of Lost Souls was, after all, a haven for children in a world of grown-up pirates and King's Men. Children like Liam and Ronagh, whose father, one of the king's captains, had left them at a nasty boarding school where they went to bed hungry each night. Children like Gil and Lucas, who had worked on one of the king's schooners and were treated no better than Port Aberhard's stray dogs. Jem was one of them, even if he didn't know it yet. His eyes were an open book, with loneliness scrawled over every page. He didn't have to admit it aloud. His parents had abandoned him, and there wasn't a Lost Soul on board who didn't understand that feeling.

But one part of Jem's story remained untold, although Scarlet thought she could fill in the blank herself. "You haven't told me," she said once Jem finished, "why you and your uncle came here in the first place."

Jem seemed to shrink inside his tailored coat, as if he was hiding something in there with him. He twisted on his barrel and bit his lip.

"You came for the treasure, didn't you?" Scarlet said. "It's no big secret. Everyone's after it. That must be why they kidnapped you." Jem had fallen silent again, so she continued.

"We looked for it ourselves for a while. But looking for a treasure that no one can describe isn't exactly easy. Some people say it's a river of gold, some say a cave full of diamonds. The King's Men are sure there're jewels around here somewhere waiting to be dug up. In fact, I've even heard stories of rubies falling from the sky!" She shrugged. "But then, some say it doesn't exist at all, that the story's complete bilge."

The Lost Souls had grown weary after scouring a few coves and coming away with nothing more than bug bites and burrs in their socks. The treasure could be on any number of islands, hidden in dense forests or buried under black sand. Their interest in finding it withered when they realized how many years it would take them to search every island. Why, they'd be ancient by that time—twenty, at least. And then there was the nature of the islands themselves: the stealthy, green-eyed panthers; the venomous snakes that slithered without a sound; the paths said to rearrange themselves overnight. Just thinking of the challenges involved in finding the treasure gave Scarlet a headache.

"Except . . ." She lowered her voice. "Except, somewhere inside me, I know it exists. And I think I know what it is."

Jem looked like he was swallowing a secret. "My uncle knows . . . I mean, *knew,* too. He knew the islands like a native Islander."

Scarlet grinned. "He did, did he? Well, that's important. These islands are confusing places, Fitz. And dangerous if you're not familiar with them."

"My uncle knew what he was doing." Jem sounded a little indignant. "He even gave me a map."

As soon as the words escaped his mouth, Jem winced, looking like he desperately wanted to stuff them back in.

"That's right! The map Lucas found on you. Well, sink me! It's a map to the treasure?" Scarlet's brain suddenly buzzed with hope. Of all the treasure hunters she'd met, she'd never known one with an actual map.

Then something occurred to her. "Wait a minute. Captain What's-his-face must have ordered his crew to kidnap you and your uncle because he knew you had inside information. So why would he kill the only person who could show him the way to the treasure? That doesn't make sense."

Jem shrugged and looked away, balling his hands into fists in his lap. His knuckles went white, and Scarlet could tell he was trying not to cry. Scurvy! She'd have to remember to be a bit more sensitive to her newest crew member. Jem wasn't as accustomed to being a Lost Soul as the rest of them.

She cleared her throat. "All right, never mind that.

How did your uncle *get* the treasure map? You're sure you can trust it?"

Jem turned to her quickly. "Oh, it's the real thing, all right. Like I said, Uncle Finn spent years on these islands. He'd just discovered a certain area where he knew, he just *knew*, there was treasure. Then the Island Fever hit. He decided he'd head to the South Pacific for a while in case he wasn't immune, and he drew himself a map so he wouldn't forget how to get back there. It took him longer than he expected to return, but . . ." Jem's voice trailed off, and again he looked heartsick. He settled his chin back on his fist and stared out at the sea.

Scarlet simply *had* to see this map. If it was indeed genuine and accurate, the Lost Souls might make hunting for treasure their mission again—this time with a real hope of finding it! But then, if Jem's uncle had risked death to keep it from the pirates, why would Jem share the map with her? And how could she keep him on board if he knew the way to the treasure and refused to tell?

They sat in the darkness for a minute or two, looking anywhere but at each other. Nearby, Smitty launched into a new tune, and Ronagh began to dance a reel in the lantern's trembling light. The *stamp-patter* of her boots on the deck only heightened the silence between them.

Knowing she was taking a great risk, Scarlet summoned all her nerve and asked quietly, "Can I see the map?"

The few minutes during which Jem didn't answer felt like one of the longest, most awkward silences she'd ever experienced. She'd just decided to revoke the question and abandon the boy on the nearest sandbar when he cleared his throat.

"I've been thinking," Jem began, still staring out to sea, "about how long Uncle Finn waited for this opportunity. I mean, he's my uncle. And . . . as much as I really just want to go home, I feel like I should, you know, finish what he started. Plus, I don't have the money to get home by myself. But if we found the treasure, I could use the reward . . ." He took in a big breath and swallowed hard. "So how about this. I show you the map, and we'll follow it to the treasure together. If we find it, we'll share it. What do you think?"

Scarlet's stomach turned a somersault. Another chance to find the treasure! Another chance to fulfill her original mission! Her heart swelled with admiration for the brave boy beside her, who'd just lost his uncle but was going to do a most honorable thing. She straightened up. "The Ship of Lost Souls," she said, trying to sound captainly, "exists to help children. Of course we'll help you. You can join us until we find the treasure, and even after that, you're welcome to stay. Crew members usually stay on board until they're grown up—" Here Jem began to turn pale, so Scarlet hurried on. "But we'll make an exception for you. If you still want to leave after this mission, the Lost Souls will help you find a way home. It's a deal, Fitz."

She held out her hand and, finally, he took it. The boy even ventured a small hint of a smile. They shook firmly, like sailors, then turned to watch the party. Ronagh's tapping boot heels had slowed, and the younger pirates'

eyes were beginning to droop in the lamplight. But no one wanted to make the first move toward the hammocks below deck.

After a minute or two, Jem nudged Scarlet's arm.

"What's your story, McCray?"

CHAPTER FIVE

These days, as hard as she tried, Scarlet could only remember a pair of hands. Long, delicate fingers twining around Scarlet's own. She could no longer picture the person connected to them—not her eyes nor her hair or even her arms. Two slender hands had become Scarlet's only memory of her mother, and she held on to them fast.

She studied Jem Fitzgerald for a moment, wondering how much of her story to offer up. She'd known him for barely an hour, but already they'd made a deal that could help them both greatly. He looked earnest enough, and for a moment she thought she *might* trust him. But then, Jem had Old World stamped all over him, and in Scarlet's experience, Old Worlders just didn't understand. She decided instead to tell him what she'd told the rest of the crew—no more, no less.

"My mother died when I was five," she said, "and my father, an admiral with the King's Men, left me with a governess in Jamestown."

Jem frowned. "I'm sorry. What did she die of?"

Scarlet swallowed. "The Island Fever."

Jem's eyes widened. "Really? Then she was one of the Old Worlders who weren't immune."

"Um . . ." Scarlet shifted on her barrel, hating this part of the story and hoping to steer away from it as quickly as possible. "It was a long time ago, so I don't remember much. My father didn't like to talk about it."

That was an understatement. After Scarlet's mother passed, Admiral John McCray had completely refused to revisit the past in any way. A friendly, comfortable sort of man before the tragedy, he practically turned to stone immediately after. At five years old, Scarlet wondered who this man was who'd taken over her father's body. She knew it wasn't him inside. The real Admiral McCray would not have hired someone like Scary Mary to be his daughter's governess.

Mary Lewis, Scarlet informed Jem, was a crotchety, leathery-skinned, pointy-toothed woman. On her good days, she was simply a grouch. On her bad days, she'd mutter incessantly to someone named Mad Linus O'Malley and pull out the hairs on her head one by one.

Late at night, in the boarding-house room they shared above a grimy Jamestown alley, Scarlet would lie in bed and listen to Mary hunting around in her old travel bags and whispering about how she needed the skin of a coral snake and the front tooth of an unsuspecting child. Scarlet had no doubt that the woman was a witch, and while Scary Mary never cast a spell on her directly (although Scarlet caught her several times looking covetously at her front teeth), she certainly made Scarlet's life scuttle.

And yet, Scarlet could never convince her father that the old woman was, at the very least, not the best person to be put in charge of her education. Admiral McCray never saw Mary's scary side. He spent weeks at a time at sea, and whenever he'd visit, Mary would curb the hair-plucking, replace her snarl with a smile, and gush about his daughter's progress. Scarlet knew that Mary needed her father's money too badly to let him see her weirdness. And he needed a governess for his daughter too badly to pay much attention. Governesses were rare commodities in the port towns.

Jem tilted his head to the side as if trying to decide whether he believed Scarlet's story. She could practically hear the questions piling up in his brain.

"So how did you end up here?" He gestured to the ship.

The other pirates had now ended their party and were wandering, one by one, down to the cabins. Scarlet watched them totter off and, for once, wished she could be sent to bed. Telling her story always made her tired.

"I ran away," she answered finally. "I was nearly eleven and couldn't take it anymore. Fortunately, Ben Hodgins found me. He was the captain of the *Margaret's Hop* back then, you know. A great leader." She hoped her voice sounded frank and businesslike, without a trace of wistfulness. "I should tell you the story he told me," she hurried on. "When I joined the Ship of Lost Souls, it had already been sailing around the islands for about eight years, ever since a ship of students got caught in a hurricane and disappeared. Turned out they survived, although the few grown-ups on board weren't so lucky."

"Why?" Jem asked. "How'd they die?"

"Oh, I don't know. Tossed overboard, maybe. Blimey, you ask a lot of questions."

"I know." He didn't seem at all remorseful.

"The children soon learned that their ship had become

a legend—a ghost story—since they'd all been presumed dead. Well, they thought that was just grand, and they took advantage of it, swooping down to frighten pirate and naval ships, pocketing some food and supplies, and feeling right proud of themselves. They found life on the *Hop* much jollier than life in port, and they decided to make the ship a home for all children who needed one.

"The Lost Souls made it a rule that when a crew member turns eighteen, he or she must move on. But most leave before that to work on the islands or go back to the Old World. A few have even gone on to join grown-up pirate ships. But that's a tricky business, because they're sworn to secrecy and can never reveal our identity—even if the Lost Souls raid their ship."

"How do you know they'll never tell?" Jem asked.

"We don't, really," Scarlet admitted. "But everyone takes an oath when they leave. Want to hear it?"

Jem nodded, and Scarlet cleared her throat and put her hand over her heart. She motioned for Jem to do the same.

"Repeat after me. Though off I go into the world to find my destiny . . ."

"Though off I go into the world to find my destiny . . ."

"I'll keep the secret of the *Margaret's Hop* inside of me."

"I'll keep the secret of the *Margaret's Hop* inside of me."

"And if I'm ever tempted to reveal that mystery . . ."

"And if I'm ever tempted to reveal that mystery . . ."

"May I meet the rope's end with a thousand lashes

until I think better of betraying the Lost Souls like the filthy bilge rat I am."

Jem blinked. Then he muttered the last line and moved an inch or two away from Scarlet.

"Now," Scarlet continued, "the Ship of Lost Souls had a purpose, as a haven for children who didn't want to live in port or with grown-ups. But the Lost Souls needed more to do than just drift around. They decided that every few years a new captain would take over and declare a new mission for the crew. When I joined, Ben Hodgins's mission was to keep both pirates and the King's Men in check as they searched the islands for the treasure. They're certain they'll find heaps of gold or jewels if they just keep cutting things down. Ben's goal was more to frighten rather than to rob them of their bounty like other pirates would."

"Hm." Jem contemplated this. "So what's your mission as captain?"

She'd known it was coming—the question she'd been asking herself so often lately. It was complicated. When Ben left less than a year ago, she decided the new mission would be to find the legendary treasure. But when the crew tired so quickly of that, she'd had to find another one, and fast. She settled on one similar to the Lost Souls' original purpose: to help children throughout the islands. But it was a tricky mission to take on—not least of all because, well, very few children actually lived on the islands. It wasn't long before the crew started having doubts of their own. She'd heard whisperings now and then from Lost Souls who were growing impatient, and she couldn't help but wish they'd just found the darn treasure. No one would dare question the captain who'd led them to it . . . whatever it was.

Scarlet forced a yawn. "How about we continue this tomorrow? I'm pooped. I'll show you to your cabin." Without waiting for Jem to reply, she hopped off her barrel and headed downstairs.

After leaving Jem to find an empty spot on the floor in the room Smitty shared with nearly a half dozen other boys, Scarlet tiptoed down the hall to her own closet-sized nook, which she shared with Ronagh. The younger girl was already curled up in her hammock, swaying gently as the ship rolled over the waves. Scarlet hopped into her own hammock and closed her eyes, exhausted but not yet ready for sleep.

She could have told Jem more; he'd probably ask for details one of these days, anyway. So full of questions, that one. But she didn't like telling anyone much about herself. Both Scary Mary and Admiral McCray had long ago advised her to forget, and although she'd resisted at first, her memories soon blurred around the edges, some of them gradually dissolving altogether.

Scarlet flipped onto her side and listened to the rafters creak as her hammock swung back and forth. Memories of her father remained, but not the ones she wanted. She wanted to picture him without his heavy, blue coat, when his skin was tanned and his face was creased from laughter instead of frowns.

After her mother died, her father barely spoke, much less smiled. He never called her by the name her mother called her, which Scarlet couldn't for the life of her remember. In fact, he seemed to want to distance her from her past and from the land they lived in, insisting that Mary replace the island maps Scarlet liked to study with a big book on Old World geography. By the time Scarlet was ten, she knew far more about places halfway around the world than she did about her own home.

Always eager to please the admiral, Scary Mary made it her mission to bring out the Old World in Scarlet. She curled her straight black hair and pinched her cheeks till they turned rosy. But the curls never stayed; Mary only succeeded in scalding Scarlet's scalp with the hot curlers. And Scarlet's cheeks stubbornly refused to stay pink, no matter how hard Mary tweaked them with her twisted fingers.

Scarlet stretched and yawned in her hammock as sleep began to creep up on her from wherever it hid by day. But she fought it off, suddenly feeling a need to relive her story—or as much of it as she could remember.

John McCray would visit her in Jamestown now and then, but he never stayed long. For five years Scarlet spent her time trying to ignore Mary's mutterings while plotting her own escape. She'd steal a rowboat and row until her arms fell off. She'd bribe some port merchant to kidnap her and desert her on the nearest beach, where she'd live off guava fruit and plump red ants. Or she'd stow away on a pirate ship, then persuade the dirty buccaneers to let her stay on board. That last one sounded the most appealing.

Then, when Scarlet was nearly eleven, her father

appeared one day at the boarding house. She'd barely recognized him. His entire posture was rigid—even his face looked tight, as if he were trying to hold something back. He sat down, then stood, sat again, and then told her that he was sending her to live with his family in the Old World.

Scarlet's mouth fell open. This was not one of her escape plans. As much as she longed to ditch Scary Mary and dirty Jamestown, the thought of leaving the islands made her insides lurch. She couldn't! But could she tell him that?

Her father didn't give her a chance. "Your ship will sail a week from today," he said, then he stood and left, just like that. It was the last time she saw him.

Scarlet didn't notice Scary Mary's presence in the room until after Admiral McCray had left. The old woman regarded her thoughtfully and scratched her papery scalp.

"So Scarlet McCray shall sail away," she said. "It's for the best, you know. Well, not for me, because with you goes my livelihood. But it's just what you need. To forget."

Later that day, Scarlet marched down to the docks, unsure exactly what she was looking for, but certain she needed to get out of Jamestown immediately to avoid this ship bound for the Old World. She sat down on the edge of a dock and swung her legs over the water. She wished she could swim or at least drift effortlessly like the flotsam that bobbed near her feet. An ara circled low overhead, unmistakable in its flame-red feather cloak, and perched on the post of a nearby pier. Scarlet watched it, heartened by the sight of one of the rare birds. It cocked its head and stared straight at her, unblinking, until Scarlet could practically hear it say, "Well? What are you waiting for?"

The notion made her grin in spite of herself. "You'd better be off, too," she told the bird. "If you haven't noticed, there're a few hundred men around here who'd like to pluck you clean."

A cry brought her attention back to earth. She scanned the port until she saw him: a boy with a dusty face and ripped trousers. He looked like any other cabin boy, except that he was upside down, being held by his ankles and shaken by a King's Man who looked like he wrestled whales in his spare time.

"I don't . . . know what . . . you're . . . talking about," the boy said between gasps as he rose and fell, his hair grazing the dirt.

"Liar," the sailor sneered. "I saw you steal those coins, and I'll shake you till they fall out of your ears if I have to." He laughed and shook the boy some more.

Scarlet scrambled to her feet, her sympathy for the King's Men at an all-time low. Cheeks burning, she marched up to the man until she stood nose to toes with the shaken boy.

"Put. Him. DOWN!" Scarlet hollered up at the man, startling him so much that he stopped shaking the boy.

"Get out of here, miss," the man spat back once he'd recovered. "This boy's a thief and no business of yours."

"A thief." Scarlet rolled her eyes. "I'll show you." And

with that, she kicked his shin as hard as she could. He dropped the boy and hopped on one foot toward her, cursing.

"You little witch! You'll pay for that."

But before he could reach out and grab her, the thief-boy rolled to his feet, grasped Scarlet's arm, and yanked her out of the way.

"Come on!" he cried. Together they scampered off down the street, leaving the King's Man limping and cursing behind them.

The boy was still laughing when they stopped to catch their breath moments later. "Now that was jolly!" he said. "I owe you one. I'm Ben Hodgins."

"Scarlet McCray," Scarlet replied. She shook Ben's hand.

He was about a head taller than her, with brown eyes under a flop of dirty, brown hair. "Do you live here?"

"Yes. Well . . . I mean, that is, I'm not . . . ," she stammered, then sighed. "For now."

"So you're leaving soon?" he said.

"I plan to."

"Where are you going?"

She paused. "I . . . I haven't gotten that far yet."

Ben nodded, and Scarlet looked down at her feet. She liked his brown eyes but didn't like them studying her. "Maybe I can help," Ben said.

At first she didn't believe him—a ship full of pirate children? Impossible. But Ben insisted that such a ship did indeed exist, for he, only fifteen years old, was its captain. Still not convinced, but hopeful that he'd at least have the decency to leave her on a deserted stretch of sand somewhere, Scarlet followed him and boarded the *Margaret's Hop* that day.

Over the following months, she learned to tie knots, weigh anchor, steer the *Hop*, read the skies. She dressed like a demon and terrorized ships, praying she'd never have to board Admiral John McCray's. She made loads of new friends on board, and as the weeks turned into months, Scarlet decided that the *Margaret's Hop* was the best home she'd ever had.

Then one day, about a year later, Ben called a meeting in Castaway Cove. Scarlet stood at his side as she often did, trying not to think about the funny feeling that she'd recently begun to have in his presence. It was a feeling of gratitude, yes, but something else, too. Something that made her gut squirm. She had just chalked it up to all the fried squid she'd eaten lately when Ben began to speak. "First I want you all to know that the Ship of Lost Souls is worth more than its captain. A captain, you see, is no better than his crew. And this is the jolliest crew that ever sailed."

The pirates murmured their thanks, a little embarrassed, and shuffled their bare feet in the sand.

"But as you know, the *Margaret's Hop* is only for the young. I'm sixteen now, and I've decided it's time for me to leave."

Some pirates gasped. Some groaned. Some remained deathly silent. Scarlet felt like she'd swallowed a rock. Ben *couldn't* leave. What would she do without him?

But it got worse. Ben went on to explain that one

day, while stealing supplies in port, he'd met a girl—the daughter of a man who owned a plantation near Port Aberhard—and he'd fallen in love. A few weeks later, he'd befriended the girl's father, who'd quickly come to look upon him as a son. The family had offered to take him in and introduce him to the life of a plantation manager. And ultimately, to groom him to marry their daughter when he turned eighteen. He looked at Scarlet, grinned, and then shrugged as if to say "What's a pirate to do?"

Scarlet hated her immediately, this girl who'd lured Ben back to land from a life on the sea. Her name was probably something like Cornelia or Adeline. She probably had smooth, corn-colored hair and a very small brain. She probably thought that pirates were grimy and covered in fleas.

"As for who I'm going to name captain when I go," Ben continued, "I've given it a lot of thought. I've chosen someone very brave, someone who knows the islands well and understands what the Lost Souls are all about . . ."

Maybe Cornelia-Adeline would make Ben wear a proper coat and clean his fingernails. Likely she had an irrational fear of millipedes—

"What do you say, Scarlet McCray?" Ben was looking at her, and Scarlet had no idea why. All she could think to say was, "You'll have to cut your hair, you know." She flushed when her voice broke on the last word.

"Will you take over as captain?" Ben asked quietly, and the Lost Souls fell silent.

"Will I *what*?" She couldn't have heard him correctly.

She hadn't yet turned twelve. Granted, she was one of the older ones now that all the original Lost Souls had moved on, but—

"Captain Scarlet. Captain Scarlet McCray. Sound all right to you?" Ben was smiling.

"Me?" Scarlet flushed again. "Um, but—"

To her surprise, the rest of the pirates cheered.

"Three great grunts for your new captain!" Ben yelled. The pirates grunted accordingly, then swarmed her with congratulations.

All except one, Scarlet remembered, as sleep now spread its heavy blanket over her hammock. One who undoubtedly thought himself more suitable for the job. One Lucas Lawrence.

CHAPTER SIX

"All good pirates, come to order!"

Scarlet McCray certainly didn't look like your average buccaneer, Jem thought, but she sure had the voice of a seaman. Seawoman? Jem decided that Scarlet would probably prefer "seaperson." He'd never felt intimidated by a girl before, but he didn't fancy getting on this one's bad side. Come to think of it, he'd never had much contact with girls at all, being an only child sent to a boys' school. So perhaps all girls acted like Scarlet. But he highly doubted it.

"I said come to order!" Scarlet bellowed again. "Can everyone hear me?"

"Even if we didn't have ears we'd hear you," Smitty called back, and received a dirty look.

All twenty-three Lost Souls and Jem stood on a thin strip of coal-colored sand in Castaway Cove, a little nook on an island shaped like a question mark. The Lost Souls considered Castaway Cove their own; they could anchor the *Margaret's Hop* behind a rocky outcropping that hid her from passing ships and the crew could stretch their sea legs on the beach.

"The best thing about Castaway Cove," Tim told Jem as they waded barefoot through the sand, "is that there isn't much danger of anyone finding us here. It's one of *those* islands."

"One of which islands?" Jem had asked.

Tim turned to him, looking serious. "The kind that make even the bravest King's Man and snarliest pirate turn tail and run. Some islands are like that—just so completely haunted that no one dares touch them. So far, the King's Men have mainly stuck to the not-quite-so-haunted islands."

Jem raised an eyebrow. "But why? How can some islands feel different than others?"

Tim shrugged. "The theory is that the most haunted places were once inhabited by the Islanders, whose spirits now roam the land, scaring off invaders."

"Oh." Jem wasn't sure what to make of that. "I don't feel anything here."

"That's 'cause we're on the beach, mate. I wouldn't go inland if I were you. This"—Tim grinned, spreading his arms wide—"is the Island of Vengeful Vegetation. Don't laugh, mate, it's true. See, years ago, some of the King's Men were searching for trees they could chop down and ship back to the Old World, and they came upon one type that didn't appreciate being chopped. Apparently if you lean against their bark or let them drip sap on you, you'll start to itch, sting, and swell all at once. And if you take even a whiff of their shiny, purple fruit, there'll be no saving you. The King's Men called the trees poison palms, and the Island of Vengeful Vegetation is just covered with 'em. That's why we never go farther inland than Castaway Cove. Well, that and the giant, dagger-wielding monkeys that live in the forest."

Jem watched Tim wander off and wondered if he'd

been pulling Jem's leg. Vengeful vegetation? Dagger-wielding monkeys? Those could only exist in stories, and rather twisted stories at that. He could only imagine what Master Davis would say. And yet, he wasn't about to venture inland to challenge the theory.

"All right, crew, we've got some important business to take care of," Scarlet announced once the crowd had stopped chattering. "Today we welcome a new sailor aboard the *Margaret's Hop*. Everyone, this is Jem Fitzgerald."

"We know, McCray, we met him last night," Gil Jenkins, a small boy with a perpetually dirty face, piped up in a whiny voice. Jem recognized him as the sidekick of the hefty Lucas Lawrence, who'd seized Jem on the *Dark Ranger*. Jem was torn between feeling grateful for the rescue and resentful for the way he'd been handled. His left shoulder still smarted where Lucas had driven his big thumbs into it.

"I'm just making it official," Scarlet said with a sniff. Then she continued, "What you don't know is that Jem here is going to help us find the treasure everyone's been searching for. Jem"—she grinned, pride glinting in her dark eyes—"has a treasure map!"

"A treasure map?" The cry rose from the back of the crowd.

"Well, sink me!" shouted Tim.

The Lost Souls erupted into chatter again. Jem had gathered from conversations with Uncle Finn that they wouldn't be the only ones looking for the treasure, but he'd never expected that *everyone* would be after it.

He couldn't help but feel proud that only he had a real treasure map.

"Order!" Scarlet yelled. "The map belonged to Jem's uncle Finn, who was made to walk the plank when he wouldn't give it up. Fortunately, Jem had the map hidden in his sleeve." Scarlet gave Jem a quick look, then corrected herself. "I mean, not fortunately, but . . . you know."

"Sure," said Jem. He didn't really want to think about that now.

But the Lost Souls weren't ready to drop the subject. "They made your uncle walk the plank?" Tim asked. "Why? Why would they knock off the person who could show them the way?"

"That's what I said," Scarlet piped up, sounding a little smug.

"That doesn't make sense," Liam Flannigan chimed in. "Are you sure?"

"I . . . heard the splash," Jem muttered, really wishing that they'd change the subject.

"Maybe your uncle's still alive!" one Lost Soul suggested.

"Yeah!" another cried. "Still on board the *Dark Ranger*! We ought to go back and rescue him!"

Jem shook his head. "It's a nice thought, but—"

Ronagh Flannigan tugged on his coat sleeve, her green eyes serious. "I'd say it's more likely they'd torture him till he gave up the secret."

Her brother nodded. "Prob'ly hang him from the yardarm."

While the pirates chattered on about the possibilities and Jem grew increasingly nauseous, Lucas Lawrence pushed his way to the front of the crowd. He looked slightly smaller than he had in his demonic cloak the previous day, but still towered at least a foot over Jem, who drew himself up as tall as he could and wished, for about the hundredth time, for a bit more height. He also noted that Lucas was missing two teeth and that a pale scar sliced across the right side of his jaw.

"So what?" Lucas said, looking down at Scarlet. "Now our mission is to rescue some grown-up?" He said *grown-up* as if the word tasted terrible.

"No." Scarlet folded her arms across her chest. "Our mission is to find the treasure and help our newest crew member. That's what we do, Lucas—help children on these islands. That's the real purpose of the Lost Souls."

"That's not what we'd do if I was in charge," Lucas grumbled and shoved his big hands into his trouser pockets, where they threatened to rip the seams.

"And that's why you're not in charge. Scuttles to be you," Smitty said. "Go on, Scarlet."

A flustered look had crossed Scarlet's face, but she straightened up and cleared her throat. "If Fitz is going to join us in the hunt for the treasure, he has to be initiated." She turned to Jem. "Ready?"

"Um, all right." He hoped it wouldn't involve anything too challenging. Or embarrassing. Once, a new player on the King's Cross football team was forced to parade around the courtyard in a maid's flowery apron and head scarf as initiation. Jem had found it funny at the time, laughing with the other boys, but now wished he hadn't.

"First," Scarlet said, "you must learn the rules of the ship. Swig?" She turned to Tim, who tugged a creased paper out of his pocket and set a pair of spectacles on his nose. Jem immediately recognized them. Just the day before, they had perched, slightly crooked, on the snout of the *Dark Ranger*'s Captain Wallace.

Tim blinked twice at the paper. "That's much better!" he said, then he cleared his throat. "The Rules of the Ship. Or, How Not to Get Yourself Marooned on a Deserted Island. Rule Number One: Everyone on board shares equally in all spoils, be it money, food, clothing—"

"See, on other pirate ships," Scarlet interjected to explain, "the captain gets one and a half shares, the quartermaster gets one and a quarter, and so on. But fractions aren't fun for anyone. So on the *Hop* we share everything evenly."

Tim, who apparently didn't care to be interrupted, looked at her disapprovingly over his spectacles. "Rule Number Two: There must be no stealing from other crew members. Anyone who does will get marooned on the Island of Smelly Wild Pigs with only a coconut for company."

"It sounds bad," Scarlet whispered to Jem, "but it's only for a night."

"Oh." Jem wasn't sure what else to say. It still sounded dreadful to him.

"Three: Everyone participates in chores and everyone takes a turn cleaning the long drop." Tim added, "In theory," under his breath, with a quick glance at Gil Jenkins.

"I told you, it wasn't my turn," Gil whined.

"I'm sorry," Jem said, feeling sheepish. "Cleaning the what?"

"The toilet," Scarlet piped up loudly, turning Jem's sheepishness to full-on embarrassment. Scarlet was certainly no ordinary girl.

"Four: Pirate girls will be given the same treatment as pirate boys. Anyone who disregards Rule Number Four will receive a kick in the shins from Scarlet and be forced to clean the long drop that day."

That one passed without comment, and although Jem had never known a rule like it, he didn't dare challenge it.

"Five: No smoking tobacco and no drinking rum. We've all seen what that does to those crazies in port. Also, no fighting on board. And no pets." Here Tim peered down at Ronagh Flannigan.

She blushed deeply. "It was just a *little* monkey."

"Six: When a Lost Soul turns eighteen, he or she must leave the *Margaret's Hop* and make a life of his or her own, even if he or she doesn't really feel grown-up yet. There will be no exceptions to Rule Number Six. At eighteen, you're one of them." Tim kicked the air as if giving a reluctant pirate the boot.

"Seven: The identity of the Lost Souls must be kept secret from the rest of the world. Anyone who tells our secret will be marooned on the Island of Smelly Wild Pigs with no company at all. And we probably won't come back."

No comments followed this rule, either.

"That's it, Fitz," Scarlet said. "Those are our rules. Think you can abide by them?"

"Sure," Jem said. It sounded simple enough.

"Jolly. On to the initiation."

They moved to the edge of the beach where the forest met the sand and settled on the ground in a half circle around Jem. After making sure no poison palms stood nearby, the pirates stretched out on the ground and watched Jem expectantly. Scarlet dropped to her knees and motioned for Jem to do the same.

"Part One of the initiation," she said. "Skill-testing questions."

"You're going to test me?" Jem asked, a little alarmed. He knew very little about life at sea and next to nothing about being a pirate. Besides, it wasn't as if he'd *applied* to join their crew. Why should he be tested?

"Don't worry, Fitz. You'll do fine. Just use your head." Scarlet cleared her throat. "First question." She gave him a serious stare. "What's your favorite color?"

"My what?"

"Color, Fitz. Your favorite color."

"Um . . . blue, I guess." Why should that matter?

"Mine too!" Liam Flannigan piped up. A few others nodded as well.

Scarlet let out a "Hm" that sounded satisfied. "Next question: What's your favorite food?"

That was easy. "Christmas pudding."

"Mmmm." A soft, hungry hum rippled through the crowd.

"Least favorite food?"

"Oh, I don't know. I don't care for pig's hocks," Jem answered.

"Any thoughts on oysters?" Scarlet asked.

"Dead or alive?"

She considered this. "Either."

"Well, I've never met a live one, but dead, they taste like salty slime." He couldn't help making a face.

"Good! More for me," Smitty called out.

"Moving on," said Scarlet. "Can you read?"

"Yes, quite well."

A murmur of appreciation passed through the group. Scarlet only nodded. "Question six: You meet a talking iguana on a beach. What do you say to it?"

"What?" Jem said, without even considering the question. "Iguanas can't talk."

A few of the pirates *tsk*ed softly, and Scarlet shook her head, looking disappointed.

"Come on," Jem insisted. "That's absurd. They can't talk." These "skill-testing questions" were getting out of hand.

"Have you ever tried talking to one?" Ronagh rolled onto her stomach and rested her chin in her hands.

Jem admitted that he hadn't.

"Then how would you know?"

"Ronagh's right," said Scarlet. "Just because you've never met an iguana that understands English doesn't mean they don't exist."

Again, the pirates watched him expectantly.

Jem sighed. Better not fight it. "All right. I'd say, 'Hello, Mr. Iguana—'"

"*Miss* Iguana," Scarlet interjected.

"Now you're just being difficult. 'Hello, Miss Iguana. Your scales are looking lovely today. Fine weather we're having. Might I carry your purse? It looks cumbersome.'"

The pirates tittered.

"Iguanas," Scarlet said, looking a little annoyed, "don't carry purses."

"Just because you've never met an iguana with a purse doesn't mean they don't exist," Jem retorted.

The other pirates laughed, and Smitty remarked, "He's got you there, Cap'n."

Scarlet rolled her eyes. "All right. Last question. What do you fear most?"

Jem thought for a moment. No matter what Master Davis said about fear being illogical, he had a list of fears a fathom long. He feared being alone in this place without Uncle Finn. He feared not being able to return home. He feared everything that might happen if his plan failed. "I fear not finding the treasure," he said simply.

Scarlet nodded as if she understood completely.

"Don't worry, Fitz," Tim spoke up. "We'll find the treasure. And honor your uncle's memory."

"Thanks." They had good hearts, these pirates, even if they had been out in the sun too long.

"Ready for Part Two of your initiation?" Scarlet asked.

"Did I pass Part One?"

"We'll let you know after Part Two." She hopped up. "Come on, lazy pirates, to your feet." The crew followed suit, clustering closer together.

"Jem Fitzgerald, give us your best pirate scowl."

"My best what?"

"Scowl, Fitz. All pirates must scowl. Show him, Liam."

Liam Flannigan pulled his round face into a toothy sneer and crossed his eyes.

"Your turn," said Scarlet.

Good Lord, Jem thought. He mustered up his best glower and curled his lip like he'd seen Captain Wallace do.

"Not bad," said Scarlet. "Now give us your best pirate grunt."

"My grunt?" he repeated.

"Right."

"Um . . . ur." Jem offered what he thought sounded like a nice, clean grunt. Simple. Unpretentious.

"Come on, you can do better. Smitty?"

Smitty stepped forward and let out a deep, guttural grunt that sounded almost apelike.

"Try again, Fitz."

"Urgh."

"Better. Now give me an URRRGH!"

Jem took a breath and let out the deepest, dirtiest, rudest grunt he could. It felt surprisingly good. A few pirates clapped.

"Much better. Now your last challenge. Show us that you can spit like a pirate."

Jem relaxed. This he could do. He'd once been forced to scrub the King's Cross Headmaster's boots for nailing him with a perfect bullet of spit from a fourth-floor window—on a dare, of course. He carefully chose a target, a spindly tree trunk a good six yards away. Then he summoned his spit and fired it out between his teeth.

Bull's-eye. The spit anchored to the tree trunk with a *fwap*! A cheer rose from the pirates, and Smitty grabbed Jem's hand, raising it above their heads in triumph.

"You passed, Fitz," Scarlet announced, then turned to the crew. "Our newest addition!" They cheered louder. Jem noted that Lucas Lawrence wasn't joining in. Then he noticed that Lucas halted Gil Jenkin's cheer with a glare.

"Now just one more thing," Scarlet said.

"What?" Jem turned to her in disbelief. "We're not done yet?"

"Well, Fitz, if we're going to start out after this treasure, we're going to need some supplies. Think of this next part as more of a learning experience than a test."

The relief he'd felt moments before suddenly slipped away. "This is where the plundering comes in, isn't it?"

"Your first raid," Smitty said with a wicked grin.

"Don't worry," said Scarlet. "It'll be fun."

CHAPTER SEVEN

Jem poked his head up over the top of a crumbling brick wall, just high enough so he could survey the scene before him but not be spotted. He'd never been in Jamestown before, but it looked much like Port Aberhard. The dirt roads bustled with King's Men in uniform and less tidy-looking sailors, everyone eyeing one another warily. A few women sashayed by in poufed skirts and grimy white gloves, exchanging a few words with the scruffier types.

Jem felt unsettled by the scene, and not just because he would soon be expected to demonstrate his nonexistent pickpocketing skills in the midst of it. Something else about the port town made him uneasy. Maybe it was the dark jungle that lay just a few streets inland, which leaned up against the buildings as if to remind them that they had no place on the island. As the Lost Souls sailed to Jamestown, Scarlet had told him that at night when the streets were quiet, you could hear mournful monkeys and lonely toads calling from the depths of the jungle. Some people, she said, get so transfixed by the noise that they wander right into the trees, never to be seen again.

Smitty's head popped up beside Jem's. "Ready, Fitz?"

"I suppose," Jem said, then resolved to sound braver. He would keep his head and proceed in logical steps. Step One: Steal a pocketknife and prove himself capable of being a Lost Soul. Step Two: Find the treasure. Step Three: Trade his share of it for a meaty reward and head straight home.

"Let the character building begin," he muttered. Master Davis would be proud.

Tim's head appeared alongside Smitty's. "Don't worry, Jem," he said. "Port raids are much easier than ship raids. More places to hide if you get caught."

"Great." Jem's thieving experience had so far been limited to pocketing shortbread when his mother's maid wasn't watching.

The three boys ducked back behind the wall and crouched on the ground beside Scarlet, Lucas, and the twins, Emmett and Edwin. The rest of the crew had stayed behind on the *Margaret's Hop*. Only a handful of Lost Souls could go to port at a time, Scarlet had explained; a small group of children might go unnoticed, but a swarm would attract unwanted attention.

"All right," Scarlet whispered. Still dressed in trousers and a boy's shirt, she had tucked her hair into a cap and could pass fairly easily for a boy. "Here's the plan. The twins and I will be in charge of stealing food today. We'll head away from the docks. Lucas will go on his own for whatever carpentry supplies he thinks we need."

"Obviously," Lucas muttered, evidently not someone who enjoyed taking orders.

Scarlet ignored him and looked at Jem. "Fitz will stick with Smitty and Swig. You two"—she addressed Jem's partners in crime—"will give him pointers. Try to steal a few doubloons so we can buy a blanket and a hammock for Fitz. And Fitz, your mission today is to swipe yourself a pocketknife. All sailors need good pocketknives."

Jem swallowed and nodded. A pocketknife. Simple enough. He could handle that, couldn't he?

"All right, pirates," Scarlet said. "Meet back at the rowboat in two hours." She placed a fist into the center of their circle. Smitty, Tim, and the twins stacked their fists onto hers. Jem settled his fist on top. Last came Lucas's, with an exaggerated sigh.

"No prey, no pay, mateys," Scarlet said solemnly.

"No prey, no pay," the others chorused.

"Go smartly now, and may you die peacefully in your hammocks rather than shackled to a weight at the bottom of the sea."

"Die peacefully!" the Lost Souls cried.

"Go on now, go!"

Scarlet and the twins scurried off, deeper into town. Lucas, meanwhile, made a show of yawning, stretching, and scratching his chest before he ambled off in the opposite direction. Smitty sneered at the boy's back as he walked away.

"Forget him," Tim said, and Jem made a mental note to find out exactly why Lucas seemed so unwilling all the time. Later. Right now he had to focus on more pressing issues. Like not getting caught and shackled to a weight at the bottom of the sea.

"All right, men," said Smitty. "Follow me, but keep a safe distance. Hurricane Smith'll show you how it's done."

Tim let out a soft snort but followed, anyway. He

and Jem sauntered into the street, looking as casual and innocent as they could, while Smitty darted between bodies and buildings. His zigzagging didn't exactly make him inconspicuous, Jem thought. He murmured this observation to Tim, who laughed.

"He's just fooling around," Tim said. "To be honest, Jem, sailors in port hardly ever notice us. They assume we're lowly cabin boys or swains and only see us when we're in their way. You'll see. Doesn't do much for your self-esteem, but it makes robbing 'em pretty easy."

As they wound their way through crowds of strangers, Jem could see that Tim was right. Sailors stomped all around, sizing one another up, but never glanced down at the boys.

"What's a swain?" Jem asked. Although he'd spent two months on a schooner, there was still so much he didn't know about ship life.

"A swain's basically a servant—the boy in charge of the captain's cockboat, which takes the captain to and from the ship. It's the lowest possible rank on board." Tim gave a little chuckle. "That was me for nearly a year."

"You? For the King's Men?"

Tim nodded. "My father got me on board. He was a midshipman. Not much higher in rank than me at first. But he learned fast and became lieutenant, then captain. Too quick, you might say. The admiral—he's higher in rank than the captain, see—the admiral didn't like how Father would take me to the captain's quarters and teach me all about navigation. He sent me to another ship, where my new captain treated me like bilge." Tim's eyes grew suddenly stormy, and he shoved his hands in his pockets. "Anyhow, I escaped soon enough. Met up with these lads—and ladies. Everything's jolly, especially now that we're on our way to find"—he lowered his voice—"the treasure. We've all been wanting this for a long time."

Jem wanted to ask what happened to Tim's father, but Tim seemed done with that topic. Strange, Jem thought, how so many of the Lost Souls didn't like to talk about their pasts. He'd had to prod Scarlet to tell bits of her story, and Smitty acted like he didn't care much at all for the family he'd left.

Tim snapped his gaze back to the street. "Where's that Smitty? Call him Aloysius sometime, will you? See if he answers. Oh, there he is, the scalawag. Watch, Jem. He's about to strike."

Jem watched as Smitty sidled up to a merchant's stall just as one of the King's Men slid two doubloons across the table to pay for a sack of tobacco. There was a moment—a mere instant—when the sailor looked away to size up a trio of passing pirates, at the same time as the merchant crouched to fill his sack. At that very moment, Smitty's spindly fingers reached in and swiped their prize. A second later, the doubloons were gone, and so was Smitty.

Tim laughed and nudged Jem. "Watch." The merchant and the sailor, after they'd both realized that the coins had disappeared, immediately took off after the three pirates.

"Come on," Tim said. "Let's go find Smitty."

"Did ya see that?" The little bandit was practically prancing when they caught up with him around the next corner. "Forget Hurricane Smith. Call me Quickfingers!" He proudly displayed the coins in his palm, then snapped his other palm over the top and danced a quick jig.

"All right, all right." Tim rolled his eyes. "No time for gloating. We've got to find a knife for Jem."

"Right." Smitty pocketed his coins. "I know just the place. Follow me, lads. Follow your uncle Quickfingers." He pranced off.

Tim shook his head and followed, muttering, "Quickfingers—ha! Percival, maybe. But Quickfingers?" Jem took up the rear, hoping his task would indeed be as easy as Smitty made it look.

They stopped in front of the tavern and peered through its single cloudy window. The interior was dimly lit and nearly empty, except for a few sailors seated around a long table in the middle of the room and a few more at tables along the wall. By the disheveled looks of them, these sailors were pirates, not King's Men. The ones at the long table seemed to be haggling over a pile of coins and jewelry.

"We're not going in here, are we?" Jem asked. "They'll notice us for sure."

Smitty shook his head. "Just stick to the walls and don't make eye contact with anyone. Let's take a look around." With that, he darted into the tavern, with Tim close behind. As he, too, ducked inside, Jem couldn't help but remember the cutlass that had hung on Iron "Pete" Morgan's hip. Such a shiny and well-sharpened blade.

He wondered, just briefly, whether pirates' cutlasses were ever used to lop off the arms of clumsy thieves. Then he tried to imagine what Master Davis would do in such a situation. The obvious answer was that Master Davis wouldn't have gotten himself into such a fix in the first place.

Inside, the tavern smelled much like the one where he and Uncle Finn had dined on flying fish in Port Aberhard. Smoky and sour. Jem took Smitty's advice and slunk along the wall closest to the door.

Over at the long table, the pirates' voices rose and fell, peppered with curses and authentic-sounding pirate grunts. There was evidently some disagreement over who got to keep a giant ruby set in gold and fastened to a thick chain. It sparkled in the lamplight, and Jem found himself so transfixed by it that he walked into a chair and stubbed his toe. He stifled a cry, and Tim and Smitty both turned and raised their eyebrows to shush him.

"It's rightfully mine!" A pirate spat on the floor near Smitty's feet, and the boy took a slow step back. The three Lost Souls pressed their backs against the wall, a few yards away from the pirates.

"Yers? Don't flatter yerself, ye lily-livered lout," a pirate with an eye patch jeered. "I'm the one who cut off the man's head and plucked the jewel off his neck. It's mine if it's anyone's."

"But 'twas me father who found it in the first place, I swear! I'd know that jewel anywhere. It fell right from the sky, nearly landed in his lap, years ago. Ye've heard the tales of rubies falling from the sky, haven't ye?"

A third pirate guffawed. "Tell ye what then, Deadeye Johnny," he said, addressing the one who'd beheaded the jewel's unfortunate owner. "I'll give you this ring and a sack of doubloons for the ruby."

"Deadeye Johnny," Smitty whispered. "Now there's a grand pirate name. Think I could be Deadeye Smith?"

Tim turned with his finger to his lips, then paused and shook his head. "You've still got both eyes."

Smitty considered this, then nodded. "It's a problem, isn't it?"

Jem silenced them both with a glare.

"Don't insult me," Deadeye Johnny was saying. "A ruby's worth a hundred sacks of doubloons these days. The King's Men've torn up the islands for 'em but come up with nothin'. Except those that fall from the sky." He snorted. "This is a treasure in itself."

"Forget his offer, Deadeye," the first pirate said. "I'll give ye me knife for the jewel." And he drew out a long pocketknife with an ivory handle inlaid with delicate, silver curls. "Belonged to Cutthroat MacPhee, it did. Long, long ago." The other pirates' eyes widened as the silver curls glinted.

Smitty turned to Jem and mouthed, "A knife!"

"Obviously!" Jem mouthed back.

"Your knife!" Smitty mouthed, pointing for emphasis.

"Jem," Tim whispered under his breath, "be as quick as you can, but stealthy. Smitty and I'll distract them if you need us to."

Quick but stealthy. Quick but stealthy. Cold sweat dripped between his shoulder blades as Jem flattened himself against the wall and tiptoed—quickly and stealthily, he hoped—toward the table.

Jem dropped to his knees. The pirates were clustered at the far end of the table, so he crawled underneath the opposite end, grateful for the shadows that seemed to be keeping him hidden. He crept along the floor, his hands sinking into puddles of rum and small, scattered crumbs, then stopped a few feet away from the pirates' boots. Above, the men haggled on.

"Come on, Deadeye. Cutthroat MacPhee's prized knife for yer little jewel."

"Throw in that big sack of ara feathers ye stole from the commodore last week, and ye've got yerself a deal."

"Me feathers? Never!"

Jem glanced back at the wall and saw Smitty gesturing wildly in the shadows. His windmilling arms seemed to indicate that the knife lay right above Jem on the table.

He drew a breath and reached up, slowly, next to the pirate with the knife, praying that hands small enough to slip out of knotted rope would also go undetected under a pirate's nose. He crept his fingers along the table ledge, then looked over at Smitty again. "There!" the boy mouthed, nearly poking Tim in the eye as he pointed. "Right there!" Jem stretched his now-aching arm a bit farther . . . and his fingers connected with cool, smooth ivory.

Suddenly there was a clatter as Tim dropped a tin mug on the floor. On purpose, of course—to divert the pirates' attention. Jem clasped the knife handle and slipped it off the table, then began to back out the way he'd come.

Quick but stealthy, quick but stealthy, he chanted in his head to the beat of his whomping heart. Almost there.

Just then, his hand slipped in a puddle of rum. He looked down to right himself. And when he looked back up, his pounding heart nearly stopped. There, staring back at him under the table, with the perfect pirate scowl on his round, one-eyed face, was Deadeye Johnny. For a moment they simply stared at each other. Then the pirate's good eye blinked.

"Get that boy!" he hollered.

Without thinking, Jem rolled away from the table and toward the wall just as Smitty and Tim jumped out of the shadows, yelling and waving their arms like crazed apes. Tim knocked over two chairs, and Smitty stuck out his foot to trip one of the pirates, who was running toward Jem, yelling, "Get him! He stole Cutthroat MacPhee's knife!"

"Run!" Tim hollered. The three boys dashed to the door and out into the blinding sun.

"Split up!" Tim called.

Still clutching the knife, Jem swung to the right, just barely out of Deadeye Johnny's reach, and took off down the street.

"Which one do we follow?" one pirate yelled.

"To the right!" another answered, followed by the now-familiar *shing* of a cutlass being unsheathed.

"Blast." Jem ducked his head and ran harder, rounding another corner and hurdling a wheelbarrow full of coconuts. He dodged a group of King's Men squabbling with a merchant, splashed through a gigantic puddle, and kept running, all the while listening to his pursuers stomping behind, cursing as only true pirates could possibly curse. And to think, just yesterday he'd questioned their very existence!

Jem dove into an alley, hoping to find a place to hide, but instead ran headlong into a skinny woman with a great nest of red hair and a boa constrictor wrapped around her neck.

"Come to see Voodoo Miranda, have you, boy?" Her eyes widened and her scarf writhed and hissed.

"Um, no." Jem did an about-face and sprinted back out of the alley, just as the pirates entered it. They took one look at Voodoo Miranda, yelped, and stumbled backward over one another to get away from her deadly accessory.

In the next alley, Jem found an empty barrel and crawled inside, pulling the lid tight overhead. The barrel reeked of old rum but felt safe. Jem let out a sigh and rested his head against the wall. They wouldn't find him in here. It wasn't possible. He listened for footsteps but heard none. Safe. He ran his thumb over the pocketknife's ivory handle, now slippery with sweat. Despite everything, he couldn't help but feel proud. He'd nabbed a most beautiful knife and evaded a trio of bloodthirsty pirates. Not bad for his first time out. And it hadn't really been *that* scary. As a matter of fact, it was kind of fun.

He was just slipping the knife into his trouser pocket when the lid flew off his barrel and Deadeye Johnny reached inside and grabbed him by the collar. The pirate pulled him up, kicked over the barrel, and gave Jem a toothy leer. His functional eye twitched.

"Gotcha, boy. Now I'm going to make ye pay." Jem squirmed and tried to wriggle out of the pirate's grasp. "Oh no, ye don't," Deadeye said, pulling Jem close enough that their noses almost touched. "We're going to start by cutting off both hands with a dull blade, then move on to yer ears. Or maybe yer nose—"

Jem gave one last great wriggle and kicked the pirate in the gut as hard as he could. As Deadeye keeled over, Jem tumbled to the ground, then scrambled to his feet and took off running again.

He took back that last thought. This was not fun. Having his ears cut off by a one-eyed pirate could not, under any circumstance, count as fun. "Whose grand idea was this, anyhow?" he growled. "Scarlet . . ."

He barely noticed Lucas Lawrence as he sprinted past the boy, focusing instead on a door in a mossy brick wall. He opened it and hurtled through, praying for a safe place to hide. He found a dark corridor. Damp. Empty.

Trembling, Jem inched back toward the door and squinted through a crack in its wooden slats. Deadeye Johnny and one of the other pirates stood a few yards away on the other side of the door, looking winded as they scanned the street. Deadeye was rubbing his stomach.

Then, to Jem's great surprise, Lucas Lawrence sauntered over to the pirates. He began to speak to them as if striking up a friendly conversation with the deadliest pirates around was an everyday occurrence, like cleaning one's ears. Jem pressed his ear, which hadn't been cleaned since he left the Old World, against the crack to hear what he was saying.

"Lucas!" Deadeye Johnny panted. "Ye seen a scrawny cabin boy run by?"

Jem wasn't sure what disturbed him more—being called scrawny or the pirates knowing Lucas by name.

"A scrawny cabin boy?" Lucas repeated, lowering his voice a few notches and rubbing his chin. "There's a lot of those around, Deadeye. Haven't seen one today."

After a pause, Deadeye squinted at the boy. "Ye wouldn't be lying to us, would ye now, Lucas?"

Lucas laughed. "You know me better than that, Deadeye. If I see your boy, I'll wring his scrawny neck."

Bewildered, Jem watched as Lucas shook Deadeye Johnny's hand and pat his shoulder before the pirate stumbled off.

Jem slumped against the door and was still leaning on it a few minutes later when Lucas pulled it open. He tumbled out and looked up at his rescuer, who stood with his fists on his hips. At least, he hoped Lucas had just rescued him and wasn't about to turn him in.

"I sure saved you." Lucas pressed his hands together and cracked his knuckles one at a time. "What'd you do to them, anyway?"

Jem eyed him warily, then shrugged as casually as he could. "Stole a knife."

Lucas snorted. "Deadeye's one of the fiercest pirates around. What were you thinking, stealing from his crew?"

Jem shrugged again and touched the ivory handle in

97

his pocket, resenting Lucas for looking so smug. He'd gotten away with it, hadn't he? And he probably could have done it without the older boy's help.

"How do you know those pirates so well?" he asked instead of answering Lucas's question.

"Look, I saved you and that's all that matters," Lucas was quick to reply. "And you're welcome, by the way."

"Oh. Well, thanks," Jem said, for in a way he *had* forgotten his manners.

"You're welcome," Lucas repeated, then jerked his head in the direction opposite to that which the pirates had taken.

"Come on. Let's stick to the alleys. If they catch me with you, I won't be able to save you again. I'll have to hand you over. They'll probably take your nose first."

As they wandered through the alleys, Jem tried to find logical answers for the many questions that had sprung to mind since he'd spotted Lucas with Deadeye Johnny. Finally he asked, "So, um, pirates from different ships generally get along?"

"What?" Lucas snapped, looking down at him.

"Well, I just thought that . . . since you and Deadeye Johnny seemed to be on, you know, good terms, that—"

"Of course not," Lucas replied. "Pirates from different ships can't be friends. That's stupid. Defeats the purpose of being a pirate."

"Oh. Right. Of course." Now Jem was very confused. Because if that were true, then this meant . . .

"You know," Lucas said, "it's Scarlet's fault that you'd be missing your nose now if I hadn't saved you. I knew she was making a mistake, sending you out pillaging on your first day. I would've said something myself, but Miss McCray never listens to me. Never listens to anyone, really, even when she knows she's wrong." Lucas's hands curled into fists at his sides. "And I'm not the only one who sees that. Just between you and me, Jem, Scarlet's a terrible captain. But you've noticed that, I'm sure. You look like a bright lad."

Jem wasn't sure what to say. Scarlet, a bad captain? A little bossy, sure, but she seemed to run a tight ship. "I hadn't noticed," he said.

"Well, you will—"

"Jem! Jem!" Lucas was interrupted by the other Lost Souls running toward them, shouting and waving. "Did they catch you? What happened?"

Jem shrugged as if it'd been as easy as simple multiplication and pulled out Cutthroat MacPhee's ivory and silver pocketknife. Scarlet's eyes widened, and one of the twins gave a low whistle. Even Lucas's mouth fell open.

"Hurray, Fitz!" Scarlet cried, then hastened to lower her voice. "I knew you could do it."

"Well"—Jem knew it was only fair to give credit where it was due—"I couldn't have done it without Smitty and Tim, of course. And Lucas." Deep down, however, he suspected he could have done just fine without Lucas.

"Oh." Scarlet looked a little disappointed. "Well, good for you, Lucas. How'd you help?"

Lucas, who'd grown fascinated with the puddle under his boots, glanced up at Jem just long enough to shoot him an unmistakable warning look. "Ah, it was nothing, really."

"We'd best get back to the boat," Tim spoke up, scanning the alley.

They all fell in line behind Scarlet, and Jem soon found Lucas at his side, going on about some planks he needed to repair the hull. Scarlet and Tim glanced back at them quizzically a few times, and Jem wished he were walking with them rather than Lucas. Although he didn't always understand their logic, Scarlet, Tim, and Smitty seemed to have real friend potential.

But Lucas Lawrence? He wasn't so sure.

CHAPTER EIGHT

"One, two, three, PULL!"

With the order hollered by their captain, over a dozen of the strongest Lost Souls bore down on ropes attached to the *Margaret's Hop*'s mast. They'd beached her at dawn on the black sand of Castaway Cove for her monthly careen—a sailor's term for a good cleaning. By yanking down on the ropes with all their might, the pirates could tilt the ship just enough to expose her underside, which they could then scrape clean.

"That's it, mates! Just a little more!" Scarlet yelled from the sidelines as the *Margaret's Hop* finally gave in with a groan and flashed them her dirty belly. Like old Scary Mary at bath time, reluctant to bathe her crusty feet. Scarlet giggled to herself, picturing the woman's feet caked with the same treasures they'd find underneath the ship: barnacles, weeds, mold, and even the odd jellyfish.

"That looks jolly. Now, who's on the first cleaning shift?" Scarlet asked.

Without waiting for the order, another half dozen pirates hoisted their scraping tools like battle swords and charged barefoot into the shallows, where they proceeded to attack the *Hop* as if she were a dragon and they were noble knights. Smitty, the shift leader, rallied his cleaning crew with yet another song:

Barnacles and tentacles,
Jellyfish and seaweed,
Clinging to the Margaret's Hop,
Ready for careening.

"That doesn't really rhyme, Averill," Ronagh commented as she popped a barnacle off the hull with her knife.

"Oh, and I suppose you could do better yourself," Smitty retorted. "And Averill's *not* the name." He pried a strip of rubbery seaweed off the hull and tucked it into Ronagh's collar. She shrieked, picked up a long, snakelike piece of kelp, and started to whack her aggressor.

Scarlet laughed and joined in with her own tools. Cleaning could be such a chore, but not with these monkeys around for entertainment.

The pirates were in a particularly jolly mood that day, and who could blame them? Scarlet herself had barely slept a minute the night before, tossing in her hammock until Ronagh sleepily suggested she count sea turtles or pretend she was dead. That last one, the younger pirate swore, always worked for her. It hadn't worked for Scarlet, though, and she passed the rest of the night imagining all the exciting things that might happen the next day. For at ten o'clock sharp, Jem Fitzgerald was going to present his mysterious map to the rest of the Lost Souls. Then they would embark on their hunt for the storied treasure.

Scarlet scraped at a clump of green mold. The *Hop*

had to be as clean as possible for the journey. The more spotless her hull, the faster they'd sail. Today's meeting would be good for everyone, she thought as she picked at the mold. Finally, the Lost Souls would feel like they had a real mission, and Scarlet would feel like a real captain. Ben Hodgins had left her some massive boots to fill, and so far she wasn't convinced that she'd been doing a very good job. Ben had been so sure of himself, so capable, so much fun. Scarlet wanted to give her crew everything Ben had given her: a home, a family, an adventure, and a purpose.

If they found the treasure, surely everything would change. Legend had it the treasure would protect the finder from harm. The Lost Souls could certainly use that. And who knew how much money the king would give as a reward. They might be able to buy new boots for everyone! Or even a new ship!

Scarlet patted the *Hop*'s belly. "Not that we don't love you," she told it. "You're just . . . nearing retirement, that's all."

The *Margaret's Hop* had aged considerably in the last few years. She still sailed well, but many a worm had found a comfy home in her planks, and consequently her sides were a patchwork of mismatched scraps of wood. At this point, your average captain would start looking around for a better ship, then attack it and throw its crew overboard, thus acquiring a newer vessel. But since it would take a half dozen Lost Souls to throw a single grown-up pirate overboard, Scarlet didn't have that option.

After a half hour of scraping, Scarlet handed off her tools to another pirate, who didn't look quite so eager, and took a stroll around the ship. As she rounded the stern, she found Lucas Lawrence prying off a rotted plank and replacing it with one he'd snagged in Jamestown the day before. As happy as she was to see the boy doing such important work, she didn't like to see her newest crew member working alongside him. Since yesterday, Lucas had glued himself like a barnacle to Jem's side, and the arrangement didn't sit well at all with Scarlet.

Jem looked up from the plank he was holding in place and waved at her. She waved back and walked over. Good old Fitz. He seemed to be doing just fine, despite losing his uncle to one of the worst fates imaginable. Or so he thought. Scarlet had tried now and then to discuss the likelihood of the *Dark Ranger* pirates actually sending Uncle Finn to feed the fish when they needed him alive and able to spew his secret. She'd even suggested they go back and look for him, but she didn't push this. For one thing, it would slow the Lost Souls' hunt for the treasure. And worse, it upset Jem every time she brought it up.

Jem had the makings of a jolly pirate. She'd known that the moment he tackled her to retrieve his map. And his daring escape from Deadeye Johnny the day before only reinforced her belief. Oh sure, Lucas played a minor role in the getaway, but Scarlet would bet her only pair of socks that Jem had done most of the work. Anyway, that was no average knife he'd stolen. She'd only gotten a glimpse of it—Jem kept it deep in his pocket and seemed reluctant to let anyone breathe on it, let alone test it out—but that one glimpse had told Scarlet the knife was something special. According to Jem, the original owner's name was Cutthroat MacPhee. Just who, she wondered, was this Cutthroat MacPhee?

"Hello, Captain," Jem greeted her as she approached.

"Hi, Fitz. Lucas." Scarlet nodded at the other boy, who didn't look up from the nail he was hammering. "This looks good. Any other spots need fixing?"

"One on the starboard side," Lucas grunted to his hammer, then whacked it against the nail head with unnecessary force.

"Another rotted plank," Jem added, watching them both with unease.

For a moment, Scarlet wondered if Lucas had been talking to Jem about her. Be a good captain, she told herself. Rise above it. She forced her mouth into a smile despite her growing urge to spit. "Looks like you're doing good work. Everyone's working hard today."

Lucas let out a soft snort and met her eyes for just a moment. "Not everyone, apparently."

Jem's eyes widened, and Scarlet felt her cheeks turn red.

"I've been working as much as you have, Lucas Lawrence," she retorted, aware that the Good Captain McCray was quickly transforming into the Angry and Tongue-Tied Captain McCray that Lucas always managed to provoke. "I'm taking a break to check on my crew," she added defensively. Then she turned and stalked away.

Honestly, just who did Lucas think he was, making

a comment like that? It was . . . it was insubordination, that's what it was. And in front of Jem Fitzgerald, too. Scarlet's ears burned, and she had an urge to dunk her head into the drink right there. Or better yet, dunk Lucas's fat head into the drink.

Instead she found a flat slab of driftwood and sank down onto it, resting her bony elbows on her bony knees and staring out at the sea without seeing it. This tension between her and Lucas was nothing new—the entire crew knew to expect at least one shouting match per month. Some days they even rated Scarlet and Lucas on the intensity of their glares and the creativity of their swear words. But lately, Scarlet had noted that whenever she happened upon Lucas and his followers—Gil Jenkins and a few other boys—they immediately clammed up and smirked at their boots. Something was up, and Scarlet wanted to make sure Jem Fitzgerald didn't become a part of it, not least of all because he held the map that would change their lives.

It was hard to believe that she and Lucas had been friends once, long ago. They'd boarded the *Margaret's Hop* around the same time, and for some reason, Lucas—who even back then was a boy of few words—saw her as a confidante. He came from a very poor family. His parents had sold him as a cabin boy to the King's Men when he was nine. He didn't want to go, but his mother was expecting another child and needed the money. Sold by his own parents—Scarlet still shuddered at the thought, although she could sympathize with the feeling of abandonment.

Although they let him apprentice as a carpenter's assistant, the King's Men treated Lucas no better than the mold on the underbelly of their schooner, and he quickly grew to hate anyone dressed in blue and brass. On his first day aboard the *Hop*, Lucas told Scarlet that he was meant to be a real pirate, attacking and pillaging naval ships, seeking revenge on the men who treated him like a slave.

And so, while the boy found it jolly to suit up and terrorize ships, he never seemed quite satisfied with his job. He envied pirates like the Dread Pirate Captain Wallace Hammerstein-Whatsit and Deadeye Johnny, who didn't get scolded when they brandished their swords and who, he thought, had cabins full of stolen treasures to keep them happy.

Scarlet used to listen to him without arguing much, although from time to time she'd remind him that the ocean wasn't really bluer on the other side of the sandbar. Even on board a grown-up pirate ship, he'd be expected to share the bounty, obey the captain, and vote when decisions needed to be made. Though they looked like wild animals and smelled like rotting fish, "real" pirates were for the most part a democratic bunch.

The trouble between Lucas and Scarlet began one day after they'd raided a merchant's ship. Scarlet found the boy in his cabin, counting pieces of eight from a sack, which he'd kept for himself while they'd divvied up the rest of the booty.

"Lucas!" she hissed. "What do you think you're doing? The Lost Souls share everything evenly. You know that."

"Quit being so high and mighty, Scarlet," he retorted,

although his eyes looked scared. He dropped his voice. "Look, don't tell anyone, and we'll share the whole sack. Just you and me. No one will know."

She hesitated a moment before shaking her head. "You know it's not right. Ben would kill you if he found out."

"Found out what?" Ben Hodgins rounded the corner at that very moment. "I probably won't kill you, but you better tell me." His kind brown eyes, suddenly somber, slid from Scarlet to Lucas and back again. Scarlet panicked at the thought of Ben angry with her—Ben who'd saved her in the first place. She bit her lip and tried to keep the secret inside, but it burst out, anyway.

Ben didn't force Lucas to spend a night on the Island of Smelly Wild Pigs as punishment, but he did make him clean the long drop for an entire week and sit out the next two ship raids. Lucas stopped confiding in Scarlet and even stopped acknowledging her, except to shoot her the odd dagger glare. These escalated to cutlass glares— broadsword glares even—after Ben chose her over Lucas as captain of the Lost Souls.

Lately, it seemed he'd decided that glares weren't enough. He'd taken to disagreeing, loudly, with her orders. Almost as if he planned to mutiny. Scarlet sighed. It was all too unsettling. No one had warned her that even as captain she would feel so completely out of control.

At ten o'clock, the Lost Souls collectively dropped their tools, gave their vessel a satisfied once-over, and scrambled up the shore to the shady forest edge. They clustered in a circle around Scarlet and Jem, and the twins passed around some bright orange star fruit they'd stolen in Jamestown the day before. After rubbing it hard on her shirtsleeve, Scarlet sliced off a piece with her knife and nibbled on it. She decided not to comment on, and tried not to remember, how the twins had stuffed the star fruit down their trousers to make their getaway. But in the end she couldn't forget. She ended up burying her fruit in the sand when she thought no one was watching. Then she turned to Jem.

"Well, Fitz? Let's see it."

Jem pulled a roll of crinkled paper out of his pocket and spread it on the sand between them. The Lost Souls moved closer together, and some of the smaller pirates slipped forward for a better look. Ronagh draped herself over Scarlet's shoulders for the best view.

An island roughly shaped like a cross—or, tilted slightly, an X—sat in the center of the map. Around it, Jem's uncle had drawn all kinds of tiny numbers and letters and arrows—navigational marks, Scarlet figured. Not her forte. She concentrated on the island, which was also covered in tiny, precise directions.

In the southern and western arms, Uncle Finn had scrawled, "Jungle. Beware," and drawn little illustrations of plants that Scarlet didn't recognize but that didn't look too menacing. In the northern arm, he'd written, "Two Peaks. Danger," and sketched two jagged mountains. In the center of the cross he'd scribbled ominous things like: "Boiling Lake. Hot," "Panther's

Lair. Hungry," and "Ophidian aggregation. Keep right." Scarlet made a mental note to ask Jem what an ophidian aggregation was. She had a feeling that "keep right" was an understatement.

Then she saw the most important, most exciting part of the map—a big X etched in dark red ink near the upper-right-hand corner of the eastern quadrant. She could barely breathe for the excitement of it all.

"So what do you think?" Jem asked. "Can you take us there? I can't follow the nautical directions myself, but maybe Tim can."

Tim set his pilfered spectacles on his nose and peered down at the little numbers and arrows that circled the island like sharks' fins. He squinted, lifted the paper up to his nose, then looked skyward as if making calculations in his head.

"What do you think, Swig?" Smitty piped up from the crowd.

Tim nodded. "It shouldn't be too hard to find. Actually, I don't think it's far away."

A murmur rose among the pirates.

"Hurray!" Ronagh shouted, wrapping her arms too tightly around Scarlet's neck. Scarlet peeled them off and was about to pick the map up for a closer look when a hand reached over her and grabbed it. Lucas pulled it away and began to examine it with Gil and a few other boys. Scarlet exchanged a look with Tim. She hoped there would be no trouble.

"Doesn't look so simple to me," Lucas commented. "Look at these directions on the island. They make no sense. 'Ophidian aggre . . . something. Keep right.' 'Turn left at the *Abicatus florificus*?' What the flotsam is that?"

Scarlet wished she'd never taught Lucas to read. He always had to be such a downer, even when he wanted the treasure more than anyone.

"Um, actually, it's a Latin name for a plant," Jem said. Then he added, a little sheepishly, "My uncle was big on botany."

Scarlet almost hugged him. But instead she grinned triumphantly at Lucas.

"See? Fitz knows. He'll take us there."

"Well, I—" Jem began.

"You will," Scarlet cut him off. She'd had enough of this reluctance. She wanted her crew to be excited! To tackle this new mission with a passion they hadn't felt since Ben left.

"What are we waiting for?" Smitty jumped up. "Let's get to the treasure!" The Lost Souls cheered. Good old Smitty. Scarlet could always count on him to rally the crew.

"To the treasure!" Scarlet scrambled to her feet and plucked the map out of Lucas's hands, ignoring his scowl. She passed it back to Jem, whose face had also brightened.

"To the treasure!" the pirates chorused.

The wind whipped Scarlet's hair into a small tornado atop her head as the *Margaret's Hop* bounced over turquoise waves toward their destination—the mysterious X-shaped island that might well harbor the storied treasure they'd all dreamed about. Scarlet felt dizzy at the thought of it.

High clouds floated across the sky. So far, it hadn't been a bad day. Scarlet tapped her toes on the ship's main deck, thankful that Tim had announced that the island was close by. She was also thankful to have a drivelswigger like him on board. He and a few other nautically inclined boys now clustered around the ship's wheel with the map, deciphering Jem's uncle's navigational directions.

"What? That's bilge. Where'd you hear a story like that?" Smitty and Liam appeared at Scarlet's side on deck, apparently engaged in some important debate.

"It's not bilge," Liam retorted. "I heard it from my dad and his crew, long ago. I'm sure it's true."

"Sure what's true?" Scarlet asked.

"Ah, we're just talking about the treasure," Smitty said. "Liam here thinks it's some old salve."

"A *healing* salve," Liam insisted. "One that cures snakebites and poison palm burns and all kinds of other island dangers. It even wards away evil spirits."

"That's a tall order, little Liam," Smitty said teasingly. "And I suppose if Voodoo Miranda sticks pins into your likeness, it'll heal those wounds, too?"

"All right, Smitty," Scarlet cut in before Liam's freckled face could get any redder. "If you're so smart, what do you think the treasure is?"

"Easy." The boy looked smug. "A golden conch."

"A what?" Liam raised an eyebrow.

"Picture it: a great, big conch shell, perfectly intact

and pure gold. What a treasure." Smitty looked almost hungry at the thought.

Scarlet and Liam looked at each other and shrugged. It would be quite the treasure.

"But what does it do?" Liam asked.

"Do? It's a golden conch, lad. Isn't that enough?"

"The story says the treasure will protect its owner from all harm—that the islands' dark magic won't be able to touch him. Or her," Liam added with a nod to Scarlet.

"Well . . ." Smitty's eyebrows inched toward each other. "I know if I had a golden conch, I wouldn't have a care in the world. Smelly wild pigs, island curses—none of that would bother me."

By this time, their discussion had attracted the attention of some other pirates who'd wandered over to listen. Among them, Scarlet noticed, were Lucas and Jem. Jem looked like he wanted to say something, and Scarlet realized that he'd never told her exactly what his uncle thought the treasure was. She was about to ask him when another pirate cut in.

"I think it's an amulet," Monty, a boy with gigantic feet, said. "Encrusted with jewels and set in gold. An amulet's meant to protect, isn't it?"

The pirates considered this and agreed it was a possibility.

"Well, I heard it's an ancient sword that can slay any monster on land or sea," Sam, a boy who had constant sniffles and breathed through his mouth, cried, brandishing an imaginary sword in his neighbor's face.

"What do *you* think the treasure is, Scarlet?" Liam turned to her.

Scarlet was quiet for a moment, sensing all eyes on her. She had a theory based on something she'd learned long ago, although she couldn't say who had told her. Her father, maybe, or one of his men. But she'd never voiced it before for fear it would come out sounding silly.

"What *do* you think, Captain?" Jem asked, and the earnestness in his voice encouraged her.

"I once heard," she began quietly, "that some Islanders used to make special trips to a sacred place where they'd dust themselves in spices. The spices came from the jungle and smelled wonderful, sharp and sweet at the same time." Scarlet could practically taste them, almost as if she'd been there herself. "The spices made the Islanders feel like they were protected. So I think"—she paused—"the treasure's a magic spice."

Here, Scarlet stopped and bit her lip, anticipating laughter. But the pirates stayed quiet, looking contemplative.

"A magic spice," Smitty said. "I like that. It's almost as good as a golden conch."

"I think it's rubbish," Lucas spoke up. Scarlet could have kicked herself for saying anything around him. "A handful of spice isn't a treasure," the boy continued with a sneer.

"You could find that anywhere. What a waste that would be. There's only one true treasure, and it's money and jewels. All the real pirates and King's Men know there're jewels around here somewhere. Lots of 'em think the treasure's a big cache of rubies. And I think so, too." He glanced around at the others, then looked back at Scarlet and added, "You're not thinking like a pirate."

Indignation surged inside Scarlet's chest. "And maybe you're just plain not thinking, Lucas. Because the legend says that the treasure will protect the finder from dark spirits and magic. Money and jewels can't do that."

"They can so," Lucas shot back, taking a step forward.

"Can not." Scarlet matched his step and glared up at his blockish head. They stood for a moment, shifting with the waves that rolled underneath the *Margaret's Hop*.

"Ahem." Smitty cleared his throat. "Ahem . . . anyone else got a theory?" He looked around nervously. "Jem?"

"Yes. Jem." Scarlet dragged her gaze away from Lucas and settled it on Jem. "What do you think the treasure is?"

Jem opened his mouth, shut it, opened it again, and said, "I think—or rather my uncle thought—" just as a cry floated over from the poop deck. They all turned.

"I said thirty degrees to the north!" Tim snatched the map from Gil Jenkins's hands.

"No, you said west," Gil cried, shoving Tim away from the ship's wheel.

"Stop it!"

"Let me steer."

"Give it here!"

"What's going on?" Scarlet yelled, marching over to them.

The boys stopped shoving, and Tim adjusted the

spectacles on his nose. "Sorry, Captain," he muttered. "We're just having trouble reading this map."

Scarlet grabbed it and shook her head at them. Studying it herself wouldn't be of any help; nautical directions meant as much to her as Jem's Latin names for plants. She returned the map, now even more crinkled, to Tim. "What's wrong? Did we go the wrong way?"

Tim held the paper a few inches from his nose to study it. "I—I don't know."

"That figures." Lucas, who had followed Scarlet to the poop deck, reached over and snapped the map out of Tim's hands. "We can't let just anyone navigate this mission. I say—"

"I can navigate just fine, Lucas. Give that back!" Tim lunged for the map, but Lucas held it high above his head so Tim couldn't reach it.

"Lucas, stop it," Scarlet began, but before she could decide whether to stomp on his toes or poke him hard in the belly so he'd drop the map, Lucas took a step backward and stumbled over a coil of rope on the deck. As he fell, he lost his grip on the map, and the wind snatched it up, lifting it high above their heads. The Lost Souls gasped as the paper flapped above them like a bird, then drifted toward the starboard side of the ship.

"Catch it!" Scarlet yelled, and the Lost Souls shuffled to the right without taking their eyes off the map.

The map changed course, drifting toward the port side of the ship. "Port side!" Tim cried, and the Lost Souls shuffled to the left, arms in the air. "Make up your mind!" he yelled at the map.

Then the map dove back toward the right, and Tim, Scarlet, and Lucas all leaped for it at once. Lucas, the tallest, touched it first, but he fumbled and fell again. Scarlet and Tim lunged for it, but Tim's elbow ended up in Scarlet's face and her knee in his stomach. They both wound up in a heap on the deck.

Jem stepped over them and caught the map as it drifted down again. Smoothing it against his shirt, he turned to the three on the floor. Scarlet looked up at him, and his angry eyes made her stop flailing her legs to untangle herself from Tim.

"Sorry, Fitz," she muttered.

"This is absurd," Jem scolded them. "No, it's worse than absurd. It's stupid. We could have lost the map just now, and all for what?" He waited until the three had gotten back on their feet. "Tim knows the most about navigating, so Tim gets the map. For now." Jem handed him the paper. "Think you can do this?"

Tim nodded. "We just went a bit off course. We're not far, though."

Lucas snorted, and Scarlet glared at him. Jem was right. This was stupid, and it was up to her to get her crew back in line after the commotion.

She turned to the rest of the Lost Souls. "You heard him. It's not far. Get ready now. Gather supplies and find your boots. Someone check the rowboat. Let's be ready to go by the time the island comes into sight."

The crew hesitated for a moment. Then they all scattered across the deck, following orders.

CHAPTER NINE

By the time the Lost Souls finally dropped anchor off Island X (as the crew had taken to calling it), it was already late afternoon. Even Scarlet, as she cursed their brief meander off course, had to admit it was probably too late to start out on a hunt for treasure. They'd have to sleep aboard the *Hop* and get an early start the next day. To fill the restless hours, some Lost Souls held spitting competitions while others debated who had the best theory about the treasure's identity. No one slept much that night.

The next morning, the Lost Souls stood on the shore of Island X, adjusting water canteens, squeezing their feet into boots, and swinging their cutlasses and rusty daggers at imaginary fiends.

"All right," Scarlet said to them, relieved to see that their enthusiasm hadn't faded, despite the delay. "I'm as eager to get there as all of you, but we should go carefully. The first part of this hike takes us through the jungle, and that means things like poison palms, snakes, maybe even smelly wild pigs."

"We'll take 'em!" Elmo, a pirate known for his ability to walk on his hands, turned a cartwheel. A few others *hurrah*ed and kicked at the sand.

They stood on the western shore of Island X's south arm, exactly where Jem's uncle Finn had indicated they should anchor, in a secluded bay with calm waters. The hike to the actual red-ink X would be a long one, but the morning was still young and warm. Scarlet chose to ignore the charcoal-gray clouds gathering over the great green hills farther inland. This island was one of the lushest she'd ever seen; the jungle rose straight up from the beach, coating the seemingly endless mountains and choking the passes in between.

A bright-red ara dove down from the sky and alighted on the beach. It tilted its head and studied the Lost Souls, then scratched at the pebbles with its beak. The sight of the bird filled Scarlet with hope. Taking it as a sign of good luck, she pulled out the map.

The route looked pretty straightforward: through the jungle and up the first ridge, over a peak, then down the other side into a valley, where they'd find, according to Uncle Finn's scribbles, an actual boiling lake. At that point, they'd be over halfway there.

From then on things looked a little muddier—more directions like "Left at the *Purpurea Atropicus*" and funny little illustrations that Scarlet assumed would make sense once they got there.

For now, there was no point in dallying, not when her crew was bubbling with energy. She rolled up the map and motioned for Jem to join her, hoping to keep him away from Lucas Lawrence. "All right, pirates. I'll lead, and Edwin and Emmett'll take up the rear. Everyone else, single file. Let's go!"

All twenty-four Lost Souls tramped into the jungle and immediately found themselves surrounded by tangles of green vegetation. Ferns of all shapes and sizes, from spiky ground-cover ferns to tall, leafy tree ferns, leaned in from all sides. A thick, green canopy closed in overhead. All this green shut like a door behind them and made a near-impenetrable curtain in front of them.

Scarlet stopped. "Um, who's got the machetes?" she called back, feeling a little silly for forgetting. A few pirates charged to the front of the pack with their weapons, looking all too eager to put them to use. "Right. You two go in front. Jem, you've got the compass, don't you? Good, you'll keep us heading north. All right, crew, minor delay. Let's get moving again."

They fell in step behind the machete-wielding boys and trudged deeper into the forest. Above the sounds of their swishing machetes and chattering voices, a chorus of insects and birds chirped and twittered like a tiny orchestra of rattles and slide whistles.

"It doesn't look like anyone's been here for a long time—if ever," Ronagh whispered, a few steps behind Scarlet.

"I know!" her brother Liam agreed. "Think it's one of . . . *those* islands?"

Scarlet turned and shook her head. The crew certainly didn't need to hear *that*. "I'm sure it just looks untouched. If it were one of *those* islands, we'd feel it right away." She spoke with what she hoped sounded like confidence, although she'd been wondering the exact same thing.

Smitty decided, after about a half hour of walking, to rally the troops with a new song. He cleared his throat and proceeded to drown out the forest's own symphony.

They've always said, "X marks the spot."
We know it must be true.
And so we trek through jungles wild,
A-following the clues.

March, two, three, four.
March, two, three, four.

There may be snakes in every tree
And spiders on the ground,
But how could we stay home when there's
A treasure to be found?

March, two, three, four.
March, two, three, four.

We aren't afraid of anything
We might meet on the route.
Except perhaps the panther's lair,
Which we won't think about.

March, two, three, four.
March, two, three, four!

"Ow!" Tim's cry interrupted Smitty's song. "What the flotsam?"

Scarlet halted without warning and found nearly two dozen pirates piled behind her.

"You might want to give us some warning before you do that." Jem sounded exasperated as he peeled Ronagh off his back.

"What's wrong, Swig?" Scarlet called back to her second in command.

"Scurvy!" came the reply. "I've been burned!"

Instantly, the pirates were clustered around Tim, staring at a patch on his hand that had already swollen to the size of a lime.

"What happened?" Scarlet cried.

"Poison palm," Tim said through clenched teeth. "It must have been. I felt something drip on my hand, then the next thing I knew, it was hurting worse than the time Smitty dropped the anchor on it."

The pirates huddled closer together and cast suspicious glances up at the canopy. Jem took the map out of his pocket and studied it, eyebrows arched. He cleared his throat. "Maybe . . . maybe we ought to consult the map more often," he suggested. "This area's called Poison Palm Paradise Jungle."

Tim snorted and wriggled his fingers, wincing.

"Can you go on, Swig?" asked Scarlet, trying not to stare at the pulsing ball on her friend's hand.

Tim grimaced and nodded. "I'm going on. I'm sure the swelling'll stop soon."

"Well, all right," said Scarlet, uncertain but not wanting to stop. "Everyone, keep your skin covered. And don't look up while you walk." Unable to think of any other precautions, she made sure Tim's hand was well bandaged in a handkerchief, then motioned the crew on into the forest.

After that, they moved more tentatively and with quieter musical accompaniment. Scarlet couldn't help but note that the bird and bug orchestra was beginning to sound less cheerful now. There were more hisses and fewer chirps. Or maybe that was just her imagination.

No, she decided after walking for another half hour, these were not ordinary jungle noises. Another voice had joined in the treetop ensemble. It was a soft moan, rising and falling and sounding almost human. At times Scarlet swore she heard it speaking, although the words were indecipherable.

She glanced behind to see if anyone else had heard the voice. Most of the pirates had their eyes fixed on the amber earth beneath them.

"Jem," she murmured.

"Hm."

"Do you . . . do you hear something odd?"

"Odd? I hear forest noises. They're a little creepy, but I don't know about odd."

"Right. So nothing that sounds like, oh, I don't know, a voice?"

"A voice?" Jem shot her a funny look. "Only Smitty singing, if you can call it a voice. Why?"

"Um, no reason. Must be the effects of the sun." Scarlet shot a quick glance at the tree canopy. "Or lack of it." She wouldn't say another word. She couldn't have them thinking their captain was going loony.

Could this mean, she wondered, *that Island X really is one of* those *islands?* She found the thought both frightening and exciting. Frightening because it could spell boatloads of trouble, perhaps in the form of vengeful Islander spirits. But exciting because even the bravest pirates and King's Men avoided *those* islands, which meant that they'd never been thoroughly explored. Scarlet had often wondered if the treasure was hiding on one of *those* islands, but she hadn't been able to convince the other Lost Souls to venture onto one with her.

They'd been walking for a few hours when the terrain started to climb and those blasted charcoal clouds began to spit. The rain fell lightly at first, tapping on the leafy roof the way it tapped on the deck above their cabins at night. But soon it was falling steadily, splashing off every leaf, dripping down every trunk, and turning the amber earth into oozing amber mud. Boots began to slip, and the pirates stopped talking at all while they cut a zigzag path up the side of the first mountain.

At one particularly steep point, the earth was so slick that the pirates had to grasp vines and roots to keep themselves from slipping or getting stuck in it.

"Follow my lead, crew!" Scarlet panted, determined to get them through this. "I'll find the best places to step and the best vines to hold on to—*yeowch*!!" She couldn't help but let out a screech when her feet slipped back and, in an effort to stop her fall, she planted her hand on a tree trunk covered in inch-long spikes.

"Blast! Scurvy!" she swore as she plucked each spike out of her skin. "Um, don't touch that tree," she added. Smitty looked like he wanted to say something clever but was biting his tongue. Scarlet thought this a wise move.

No sooner had they begun to walk again when another panicked cry rose from somewhere in the middle of the pack. Twenty-three soggy pirates turned once more to find Liam flailing his arms at an angry-looking black monkey who had a firm grip on the boy's hair. A few Lost Souls gasped. A few screamed.

"Get it off me!" Liam yelled. "Make it stop!"

One of the machete wielders—a stocky youth named Charlie—rushed forward with his weapon.

"Don't hurt it!" Ronagh shrieked.

"What do you mean, 'Don't hurt it?'" Liam yelled, still flailing. "Don't hurt *me*!"

Charlie gave Ronagh a withering look and, with one swift motion, sliced off a sturdy piece of vine. He swung it at the vicious little creature, who leaped off Liam with a scream and retreated into the trees.

Liam rubbed his head and watched a few tufts of red hair flutter to the ground. "Thanks," he said to Charlie, who was looking very pleased with himself. Then Liam turned to his sister. "That was all your fault! What were you thinking?"

"What?" Scarlet cried. "What happened? Ronagh?"

The smaller of the two little Flannigans looked like she might cry. "I'm sorry," Ronagh whispered. "I just . . . I saw the monkey and wanted to play with it, so I called it over and . . . and it attacked Liam." She gestured to her brother's now very red head.

"Oh, that was smart," Gil Jenkins sneered. "This is obviously one of *those* islands. What makes you think you can make friends with the wildlife?"

Tears gathered in Ronagh's pale-green eyes and mingled with the raindrops dripping down her cheeks.

"Oh, stop it," Liam said gruffly. "Ronagh, don't cry. It's all right. Let's just get going." He glared at Gil.

"Right, let's head on," Smitty said. "Just remember: Don't look up, don't make eye contact with the animals, watch your step, and watch where you put your hands." He ticked off the rules on his fingers, then tossed a teasing look at Scarlet, who managed to smile back at his joke, even though it was weak and at her expense.

The eerie voice continued to hum in Scarlet's ears all the way up the first mountainside. Now and then she'd steal quick glances at Jem, but he never showed any sign of hearing it. She sure hoped she wasn't going loony.

"Look! The trees are thinning! We're nearing the peak!" Charlie called out. Within moments, they found themselves standing atop the mountain, looking out on a vista of rolling hills cloaked in jungle. A thick, gray mist drifted through them.

The Lost Souls stopped to catch their breath and take in the view. Scarlet noticed that Jem, although never the chattiest pirate, was particularly quiet. His eyes had nearly doubled in size, and he didn't seem to care about the raindrops cascading down his face as he looked around.

"I've never seen anything like it," he murmured, perhaps to her, or perhaps to himself. Then he let out a short laugh and turned to her with a grin. "It seems," he said, "that adventures really do happen. It's not all stuff and nonsense." And he laughed again.

Not quite sure what her newest recruit was talking about, Scarlet smiled, anyway, and handed him a canteen in case he was getting dehydrated. At least he seemed to be enjoying himself.

"Where to now?" Liam asked after a few minutes. The rain was easing to a sprinkle, and the pirates were looking less peaked now that they'd ascended their first mountain.

Jem looked at the map again. He wrinkled his nose. "'Turn left at the *Abicatus florificus*'?" While all the other pirates watched, he looked around at the vegetation, finally settling on a fuzzy little stalk with a bushy pink head. He swallowed, looking uncertain, then consulted his compass.

"This way, I think." Jem pointed down the mountain's steepest side. Together, the pirates peered over the edge. This side of the mountain, splotched with amber and purple rocks and bright green moss, bore little resemblance to the jungle-covered side they'd just climbed. From what Scarlet could tell, if they made it down in one piece, they'd find themselves in a narrow valley mostly obscured by fog. Not the most inviting landscape.

Suddenly Scarlet realized that all eyes were on her. The machete boys had retreated to the rear of the line.

"Oh. Right. I guess I'm first." She gulped and shuffled toward the edge. "Nothing to it, I'm sure. Just make sure you go slow-ow-ow-ow!"

Her first tentative step down caused the amber and purple rocks beneath her boots to give way into a mucky amber and purple rock slide, sweeping Scarlet's feet out from under her and sending her sliding, heels first, straight down the mountain.

The slide was impossible to stop, no matter how hard she dug her boots into the ground. Down she tumbled, over spongy mounds of moss and not-so-spongy lumps of clay, terrified of where she might land. *Bump, bump, squish. Bump, bump, squish.* After what felt like long minutes but was probably only a few seconds, Scarlet realized that, aside from the bumps, this wasn't such a bad way to travel. She would be filthy when she reached the bottom, but it'd likely save her a good half hour of hiking. She began to relax and enjoy the ride, and the shrieks behind her told her that the rest of the crew was following suit.

Splat. All too soon the ride came to an abrupt end in a giant mud puddle. Scarlet sat up, completely caked in mud, like a life-size clay sculpture.

Splat. Splat. Splat.

Jem, Smitty, and Tim landed in the puddle beside her, whooping with laughter. All three were as filthy as Scarlet, especially Smitty, who looked like he'd slid down the hill face-first.

"Wha' a wide!" Smitty sputtered through a mouthful of mud. He spit, then wiped the mud off his eyelids so his face was just two big eyes in a goopy, amber mask. "Way to lead the way, Cap'n. What fun!"

Tim chuckled as he wiped mud from his spectacles.

Even Jem, his tailored clothes now thoroughly grubby, was laughing. In fact, all the pirates seemed to have forgotten the uncomfortable climb thanks to the ride down. Tim no longer cringed every time he moved his bandaged hand, and Liam and Ronagh giggled as they tossed mud balls at each other. Scarlet herself even forgot the voice in her head as she watched the rest of her crew hurtling down the slope into the puddle, shouting and shrieking. No one cared about a little rain now that they were the dirtiest they'd ever been.

"Well, sink me. Would you look at that?" Tim had stopped laughing and was looking around him, openmouthed. Scarlet looked up and gasped.

They'd landed in a narrow valley that snaked between the green mountains. The ground was a mosaic of brown grasses, fern tufts, and small purple boulders. But the most amazing sight of all was the steam rising in curly plumes from the ground and twirling around the Lost Souls.

"Shivers," Scarlet breathed. "Where's the steam coming from?" She scrambled to her feet.

"Look!" Tim had already discovered the source. "It's coming from these little rivers! They're all over—simmering streams!"

It was true. Milky little streams ran all around them, bubbling and burping as if heated from below by underground fires.

"Simmering streams!" Scarlet looked at Jem and he looked back, his eyes full of excitement. Simmering streams could only lead to one thing: a boiling lake!

"Hurray! We're halfway to the treasure!" Scarlet bounced up and down, then felt suddenly dizzy as the moaning voice returned to her head, louder now. Why wouldn't it leave her alone?

"So, logically, if we follow the streams, we'll end up at the lake, right?" Jem said.

Scarlet nodded, trying to ignore the voice. "Makes sense. Let's go." She needed to keep moving. "To the lake!"

On they charged, twenty-four pirates wearing mud and mad grins. They scampered through the valley, skirting the streams, which every so often would merge and surge faster toward their destination. Now and then, Scarlet wondered if they ought to check the map, but she couldn't bear to stop. She wanted it too badly—both the treasure and this wild energy the crew had been lacking for so long. And she wanted the blasted voice to stop droning. She picked up the pace. Maybe she could outrun it.

Something glimmered off to her left, and Scarlet glanced over quickly to see a patch of green wavering at the foot of a nearby mountain. It almost looked as if the trees were parting or even changing shape amid the steam. A streak of red, like an ara in flight, flashed between the trees, and the scene returned to normal. Scarlet halted and shook her head. Now she was seeing things, too? What was this island doing to her?

"What's wrong?" Jem appeared at her side. "Should we check—"

"No. Let's go." She would outrun it. The island wouldn't stop her.

The streams continued to merge and grow stronger,

burbling and steaming and spurring them on. The pirates were practically sprinting now.

"We're almost there," Scarlet huffed to Jem. "The lake has to be just around this . . . corner." She stopped suddenly, and several pirates staggered to a halt behind her.

Around the corner, the streams did indeed reach their destination, flowing into one body of water. But something was wrong. What lay before them didn't look like the boiling lake Scarlet had imagined. No, it seemed as if, at some point, the streams had ceased to simmer, terminating instead in what looked more like a shallow, murky pool.

Smitty raised an eyebrow. "Is this it?"

"It can't be," Jem said. "This isn't a boiling lake." He looked around him. "But this is where the streams end."

"It's not a boiling lake." Scarlet was sure of that. She knelt by its edge, dimly aware that the voice in her head had disappeared. She dipped her hand into the water and felt her heart sink. At that moment, the clouds decided to let loose again, and within moments it was raining with a vengeance.

Lucas Lawrence stepped forward and knelt beside Scarlet. He, too, immersed his hand, then turned to her with a sneer.

"It's a lukewarm slough," he announced. "You've led us to a lukewarm slough. That really scuttles, Scarlet."

No one else said a word, but Scarlet could feel their eyes on her and could practically taste their disappointment. A clap of thunder overhead urged the rain to fall harder. Scarlet wondered if the earth might just open up and swallow her right there, saving her from this awkward silence, this humiliation.

She put on her bravest face and looked at her soggy crew. "Let's . . . let's just think for a moment. We must have taken a wrong turn somewhere, probably not far away. If we just retrace our—"

"Retrace our steps?" Lucas stood up. "We're way off base, McCray. And it's pouring rain, and it'll be dark in a few hours. We'll be wandering around for days, and we'll probably never find it, anyway."

"But you don't know that. You have no—"

"I say we go back to the ship," he interrupted again.

Back to the ship? "But we've come so far. We can't—"

"So far, we've been attacked by monkeys and poison palms, and now we're soaking wet. I, personally, don't want to spend the night in a rainy jungle when I could be dry on the *Hop*."

The Lost Souls began to whisper among themselves.

"Wait! And stop interrupting me, Lucas," Scarlet said angrily. "We can't go back now. So what if it's raining? We've got a map to the treasure!"

"Let's put it to a vote." Lucas put one meaty hand on his hip and wiped the water drops from his forehead with the other. "All in favor of getting off this island and back on the ship, say aye."

Scarlet couldn't believe this was happening. She should have had Lucas strapped to the mast the first time he ever undermined her authority. But now it was too late—he'd finally gone and done it. He'd asked the crew to vote against her. And worse, she couldn't think of anything to say.

"Aye" came a few small voices from the rear of the group.

"Aye." A shout from Gil Jenkins.

"Aye." A whisper from Sam, the mouth-breather.

Thunder boomed again as if trying to drown out the pirates' "ayes." But Scarlet heard them, anyway—all fifteen of them. Not a unanimous vote, no, but enough to make Lucas the winner. Enough to call Scarlet's authority as captain into question.

CHAPTER TEN

The sky shone clear and brilliant blue the next day. Jem stood on the quarterdeck and glared up at it. Not a hint of rain in sight. That figured.

It was, he decided, a perfect day for a second attempt at the island that had bested them the day before. It only made sense to try again—they couldn't give up after one expedition gone wrong. What was it Master Davis used to tell him whenever math problems made him want to throw things? "If at first you don't succeed . . ."

And yet, despite his eagerness to get back out and find the treasure, Jem knew better than to suggest another expedition today. Today, every pirate on board was in a foul, foul mood.

Ronagh had whined about a tummy ache all through breakfast, then retreated to her hammock. Emmett and Edwin got in a minor fistfight over whose turn it was to clean the long drop. Smitty didn't offer a single joke on the subject—not even a bad one—and didn't even hum as he swabbed the deck.

And then there was Scarlet. Captain McCray emerged from her cabin like a great big storm cloud that morning. She ate her breakfast in silence, except to growl that someone had polished off all the fruit so they'd have to make do with jaw-breaking slabs of hardtack until they could next go to port.

Her dark eyes held an arsenal of daggers and swords, ready to impale the first sailor who crossed her. After she'd mauled her hardtack, she stomped back to her cabin, saying that she was going to look after Ronagh and if anyone so much as knocked on her door, she'd hang them by their big toes from the mast.

Jem wondered if anyone else noticed that Scarlet looked like she'd been crying.

If she had, Jem couldn't blame her. The previous day had absolutely scuttled, as the crew would say. After most of the Lost Souls had voted for warm, dry beds over a night in an inhospitable jungle, they'd had to face the long slog back to the *Hop*, under a darkening sky and rain that wouldn't let up. For hours on end, they stumbled along the trail, flinching at every monkey's cry and every unidentifiable crackle in the bushes. By the time they boarded the *Hop* and set off for the still waters of Castaway Cove, everyone had given up on conversation. Scarlet herself had stopped talking right after Lucas called the vote.

Now, under the smug midday sun, Jem felt a nasty mood of his own creeping up. All around him lay coils of rope, tangled together like a nest of long, brown snakes.

"Your job today," Tim had told him about a half hour ago, "is to untangle this mess so we can use the good ropes to replace worn parts of the rigging." With that, he'd wandered off, muttering about a throbbing pain in the hand that had fallen victim to the poison palm. Even the *Hop*'s agreeable quartermaster was in a sullen mood.

Jem attempted to find the ends of the rope, but within minutes, found himself tangled up inside the mess instead. Somehow, he'd gotten the rope wrapped around his ankles, elbows, left thigh, and even his neck.

"Scurvy! Blast! Blimey!" Jem used all the pirate expressions he knew trying to wriggle free, but he only succeeding in further entangling himself. Although he knew the rope needed to be intact to fix the rigging, he suddenly didn't care, and he fished inside his right pocket for his knife to cut his way out of the mess.

"Stupid pirates," Jem grumbled. "What do I know about ships or rigging or ropes? They should've done this themselves. Then maybe—"

Strange. His right pocket was empty. He rarely ever took the pocketknife out, since he'd gone to such trouble stealing it. He checked the left pocket. No knife there, either, only a slightly chewed wad of gum he'd left there two days ago, "for later."

He checked his coat, shirt, and boots, but found no silver-and-ivory-handled pocketknife.

"Blast!" He'd gone and lost it! What kind of a pirate went and lost his knife? Now Scarlet would probably insist he steal another. And after what he went through for this one . . .

No way. Jem folded his arms. No way would he risk his life for a stupid knife again. It just didn't make sense.

He was standing like that, sulking among the loops and coils, when Tim returned. The quartermaster raised an eyebrow but didn't comment—he only surveyed the knotty situation. Then he gave a few tugs here and there, and the rope tumbled to the ground like an obedient charmed snake.

Blushing a little, Jem stepped out of his binds and muttered his thanks. Tim shrugged and trundled off again.

Interesting, Jem thought, as he glanced around to see if anyone else had witnessed his embarrassing attempt to tame a rope, how only one person on board seemed untouched by this contagious bad temper. Lucas Lawrence. The boy had been strutting along the main deck all morning, whistling a sea chantey and grinning with all his remaining yellow teeth at everyone he passed—as if he owned the ship. Every so often, Lucas would loop an arm around some unsuspecting pirate and pull him aside to whisper in his ear. Jem gulped as he watched, hoping this wasn't what it looked like.

He left the rope and headed in the opposite direction, wanting to avoid Lucas's grin. Instead, he came upon Liam and Gil, who had been given the chore of sealing gaps in the ship walls with caulk—except that they had abandoned their task and now stood nose to nose, arguing. As Jem watched, Liam's cheeks turned from pink to red to deep crimson.

"That's not true and you know it, Gil," the boy was saying. "Tim can read a map better than anyone. He couldn't have brought us to the wrong island. There were simmering streams, remember? That means the boiling lake was around there somewhere."

Gil smirked. "Then why didn't we find it? It's not so hard to follow a map. I could've done it if he'd let me."

He sounded like Lucas, and Jem didn't doubt that Gil was quoting his much larger friend.

"You!" Liam spit on the deck. Rather sloppily, Jem noted, but still piratelike. "You can't find your way out of your own hammock without Lucas's help. So we took a wrong turn somewhere. That could happen to anyone, anywhere."

Jem started as a new thought hit him. A wrong turn. Anyone, anywhere. Maybe that anyone had been him, misidentifying the *Abicatus florificus* and sending the Lost Souls down the wrong side of the mountain. He hadn't been certain of the plant's identity, after all, having largely slept through Uncle Finn's lesson on the genus *Abicatus*.

Jem turned away from the quarrel and began to walk back the way he'd come. Could it really have been his fault they lost the treasure trail? If only he'd taken Uncle Finn's lectures seriously. Or better yet, if only Uncle Finn were there with them now.

But he isn't here, Jem told himself, and not for the first time. He resigned himself to Uncle Finn's death, and yet couldn't help but wonder, every now and then, if the Lost Souls had a point. Would the pirates really kill off someone who knew where to find the treasure? Still, he couldn't allow hope to rise above logic. He'd heard the splash. Uncle Finn was gone.

"Jem! Just the man I've been looking for." A heavy arm settled onto Jem's shoulders and tightened around his neck like a boa constrictor. Jem's knees buckled momentarily, and he slid his gaze sideways to Lucas's yellow grin.

"Come," the older boy said, steering him toward the

ship's starboard side. "We have to talk. Man to man."

Jem felt minuscule under the weight of Lucas's arm. They stopped at the railing and looked down on the milky blue waves that lapped lazily against the *Hop*. Some fifty yards away, Castaway Cove and the Island of Vengeful Vegetation wavered in the midday heat.

"It was an embarrassment, wasn't it?" Lucas launched right in. "Yesterday, I mean. We had a map and twenty-four able pirates. There's no excuse for what happened. We should all be rolling in treasure right now."

Jem opened his mouth to speak, hoping to lighten the mood with something wishy-washy like, "Accidents happen," but before he could say anything Lucas went on.

"And you"—the boy turned to face him—"must be especially mad. You should be on your way back to the Old World by now."

Jem let himself imagine that—going back to school, to mathematics and grammar lessons, to always knowing what would come next—for just a moment before tuning back in.

"I've had enough of this bad leadership," the boy was saying. "And others agree. There's a good lot of us, and we're prepared to"—he lowered his voice—"mutiny."

Jem's stomach pitched as if the sea had suddenly turned stormy.

"I'll be captain," Lucas said. "And real deserving pirates, like yourself, will stand at my right hand, at least until we find the treasure and you head home. What do you say?"

"I . . . um . . ." was the most intelligent response Jem

could come up with. What a mess this was turning out to be. Scarlet might have a mutiny on her hands, when he might well be at fault for the treasure hunt gone wrong! He had to tell her. She couldn't shoulder all the blame. But then, if he confessed to a possible blunder, he might just end up strung up by his toes from the mast.

"I . . . don't know," he concluded.

Lucas straightened and bared his teeth in what Jem guessed was meant to look like a winning smile. "Think about it, then. I'll give you till sundown." He withdrew his arm, began to move away, then turned back. "You're a good man, Jem," he added. "I know you'll make the right choice."

CHAPTER ELEVEN

"Fitz, you look downright sick," Smitty commented when he found Jem sitting cross-legged on a barrel on the quarterdeck. "In fact, you look like you just might spew. Is it the hurricanelike conditions?" Smitty swept a hand out over the sea, which barely rippled under the late-afternoon sun. The *Hop* was still firmly anchored off the shore at Castaway Cove. "Or perhaps all the treats we ate for breakfast? Pudding, jelly, chocolate cake . . ." Smitty was grinning. Of course they'd only had hardtack. But at least one pirate's bad mood seemed to be wearing off. Jem, on the other hand, felt like he couldn't sink any lower.

"I'm fine," he said to his feet. "Just a little . . . under the weather." He couldn't tell Smitty what he'd just learned from Lucas. He had some thinking to do and very little time in which to do it.

"Well, we're all a little out of sorts today," Smitty said. "Some more than others." He jerked his head toward the staircase leading down to the cabins. "But it's only fair to warn you that Mad Scarlet McCray means business today. If she catches you lolling about when there's work to be done, well . . ." He pointed to the mast above their heads. Although Smitty's eyes gleamed with laughter, Jem decided not to take any chances. He slid off the barrel.

"Come on. We could use another hand with the

rigging." Smitty turned and walked toward the main deck, and Jem followed, still tangled in his own thoughts.

I know you'll make the right choice, Lucas had said. The right choice. He made it sound so simple, like choosing between flying fish or oysters for dinner. But Jem knew better. He didn't trust Lucas—the way the boy talked about other sailors behind their backs, the way he couldn't stand to take orders. And what happened during the knife-pilfering lesson still smoldered in Jem's brain.

And yet, Jem couldn't forget his own mission. His best interests lay with the captain who could get him to the treasure. Scarlet had drive and enthusiasm, but Lucas . . . Lucas had something else. Jem sensed it in the way he moved about the ship. Lucas wanted the treasure with an intensity all his own. And that could work to Jem's advantage.

He and Smitty joined a group of sailors puzzling over the ropes that had defeated Jem earlier in the day. Tim was instructing Liam, Edwin, and Emmett on how to replace the worn cordage, or ropes, on the rigging high above them.

Jem hung back. Master Davis would say "The end justifies the means." Therefore, it made more sense for Jem to side with Lucas so he could reach the treasure as quickly as possible and go home.

Jem turned back to the crew and saw Smitty creeping around the other boys, winding a rope around their ankles as they deliberated who would climb the mast to replace the old cordage. Elmo, their usual crow's nest lookout man, was in bed with a cold and couldn't manage the climb. Smitty looked up, caught Jem's eye, and winked. None of the others noticed his stealthy work.

After winding his rope around the boys two more times, Smitty waved at Jem and, with the wickedest smile Jem had ever seen, gave the rope one swift tug. The boys yelped as they were jerked together at the knees, then toppled backward in perfect unison. Jem forgot his conundrum and let out a hoot, while Smitty danced his victory jig.

"Did ya see that?" Smitty crowed. "That was the handiwork of Sneaky Smith, Terror of the High Seas, the most—"

"Argh!" Tim scrambled to his feet and threw himself at the prancing pirate.

"Take that, Wilfred!" Emmett barreled into the pair, and soon all the boys were piled on top of Smitty, tying his legs and arms together.

Jem fell quiet as he watched. Siding with Lucas would mean siding against these sailors and against their captain, who had not only witnessed his kidnapping and commanded a rescue, but had promised to take Jem to the treasure. They'd shaken on it. And despite Scarlet's rather unladylike habit of threatening to kill people, she was his friend. He trusted her. But could he base such an important decision on that?

Smitty emerged from the pileup, swathed in rope like a mummy and tipping from side to side, his legs bound together. At that moment, Scarlet and Ronagh came up the staircase and froze, mouths open. The boys stopped laughing, waiting for Scarlet's reaction. But rather than lambaste them for slacking off, Scarlet doubled over laughing.

In that moment, Jem knew for certain that these sailors would not desert their captain. Not for Lucas, not for treasure, not for anything. These Lost Souls would say that Master Davis was wrong: The end couldn't justify the means if the means involved deserting your captain and friend. And as he watched them all whoop with laughter, Jem had to agree. He wouldn't side against them. So Master Davis was wrong. And not for the first time, either; he'd also said that adventures were stuff and nonsense. So maybe, Jem mused, just maybe Master Davis's logic couldn't provide all the answers—especially not in a place like this. Maybe he needed a different kind of logic here. The logic of one who knew and understood the islands. Someone more like . . . Uncle Finn.

Decision made then. Jem shuffled over to Scarlet, who was still laughing. "Can we talk?" he asked, and she nodded, stifling her giggles. They moved away from the ruckus, which by now had attracted even more pirates. Everyone seemed to want a piece of Smitty now that he couldn't defend himself.

"What is it?" Scarlet asked, sounding much less growly than she had at breakfast.

"I've been thinking," Jem began, fiddling with his cuffs, "that *I* might have been the reason why we didn't find the treasure yesterday." Scarlet's eyes widened, and he hurried on. "I mean, I was fairly certain . . . well, maybe seventy percent certain—all right, sixty-five— that the plant I pointed out was an *Abicatus florificus*,

144

but . . . but I may have been mistaken." Scarlet opened her mouth to speak, but Jem kept going. "So I thought you should know that it . . . you know . . . wasn't your fault. You see, it could have been me."

Scarlet said nothing, she just looked at him.

"I'll go string myself from the mast now," Jem concluded, and finally she smiled.

"Don't bother. Thanks, Fitz. You might be right. We could have taken a wrong turn at the Abiwhatsit, but I . . ." She puffed out her cheeks and rolled her eyes. "I should have slowed down and read the map. Like you said." She scraped the toe of her boot along the deck, and Jem could tell she hated admitting that she had been in the wrong.

"So let's head out again and go more carefully," he suggested. "Learn from our mistakes. There's no sense in sitting here when there's a treasure to be found. Especially when we have a map."

Scarlet's lips twisted into a small smile. "Now you're thinking like a pirate!" she said. Then her smile faded a little. "Think they'll be willing to go again after yesterday's disaster?" She nodded at the crew.

"They better be. They're pirates, aren't they? Undaunted by monkeys and poison palms."

Scarlet grinned. "What about rain?"

"Well, they'll just have to get used to that."

She paused, then nodded. "All right, Fitz. I'll rally the crew at sundown. We'll return to Island X tomorrow to find the treasure."

Sundown. Jem cringed as he remembered the deadline

Lucas had given him. The sun had already started its lazy journey toward the horizon.

He had no time to ponder what sundown might bring, because just then Lucas himself arrived on deck, a small group of followers trailing behind. They eyed the rope warriors warily, and Jem wondered exactly how many of them knew about the conspiracy unfolding under their runny noses. Scarlet's smile had disappeared completely.

Once they'd set Smitty free, they returned to the task at hand: deciding who would climb up the mast to replace the worn ropes. It would have to be someone strong—Liam and Ronagh were out. And someone not afraid of heights—that eliminated Emmett and Sam. Tim pleaded nearsightedness; Gil claimed he'd sprained his ankle the day before and instantly adopted a limp.

Scarlet sighed. "Oh, all right," she said. "I'll—"

"I'll go," Lucas interrupted. "I'm by far the strongest. And I'm not afraid of a little climb." He leered at Emmett as he looped a rope over his shoulder. "What kind of pirates are you, anyhow?"

Scarlet let out a strangled sigh, and Jem wondered if now would be a good time to tell her about Lucas's plan to mutiny. Now, while the boy could more easily be strung up by his toes.

Lucas grasped a rope that hung down from the mast and pulled himself up, swinging for a moment above their heads. "I'll show you how it's done," he cried, then gripped the mast between his legs and began to climb. But just then something fell from his pocket. It glinted as it twisted in the air, hurtling down to land with a clunk at Gil Jenkins's feet. Jem knew what it was even before Lucas's sidekick hurried to pocket it.

"Hey!" he yelled, pushing his way over to Gil, who had assumed an innocent expression. "That's mine."

"What is it?" Scarlet asked.

"Nothing. It's . . . nothing," Gil stammered.

"It's my knife." Jem planted himself in front of the boy, for once taller than an opponent. "Give it back."

A nearby thud told Jem that Lucas had abandoned his performance. He could sense the older boy towering behind him but didn't want to look.

"Your knife?" Tim asked. "What was Lucas doing with it?"

"He lent it to me."

Jem spun to face the liar. Lucas stared back with an unwavering gaze that made Jem sweat.

"He lent it to me for chores this morning. Didn't you, Jem?" Lucas's eyes narrowed, and Jem saw a flash of something inside them—something other than the usual bullying. Something really menacing. He looked at Scarlet, who watched them both in silence. Then he drew a breath.

"No. I didn't lend it to him. He stole it."

A murmur surged through the crowd as everyone turned to Scarlet. She had become a shade or two paler.

"Gil," she said, "give Jem his knife."

Gil scowled, but did as he was told. After inspecting the knife for chips and scratches, Jem shoved it down into the deepest recesses of his right pocket.

Scarlet turned to Lucas. She spoke slowly, as if every word counted. "Did you steal it, Lucas?"

The crew stood so still and silent as they waited for his answer that they could have heard a minnow jump a mile away.

"So what if I did?" Lucas finally answered. "It's just a stupid knife. What are you going to do about it, *Captain*?" He smirked, but his lips quivered just a little.

"Well," Scarlet spoke slowly again, looking a little uncertain herself. "You know the punishment for stealing . . ."

Lucas's smirk wilted. "You wouldn't."

Scarlet turned back to Jem and raised her voice a little. "This pirate stole your knife, Jem Fitzgerald?"

"He did," Jem said.

"Then he must be punished," Scarlet replied, her voice filled with a confidence she didn't quite feel. "One night on the Island of Smelly Wild Pigs!"

"What?!" Lucas obviously couldn't believe his ears.

"You heard me." Scarlet's face now looked more stony than pale.

"You'll be sorry, McCray." Lucas spit on the deck and stomped off.

Scarlet watched him go, then turned toward the sun, which now hovered close to the horizon. A few mauve-colored clouds had gathered to watch it sink until the sea extinguished its flames.

Then she turned to Tim. "We're changing course. To the Island of Smelly Wild Pigs!"

The crew scattered without comment. Soon they were headed west, straight into the orange sun that seemed to be trying to blind them with its brilliance.

CHAPTER TWELVE

"Do you have a ten?"

"Go plunder."

"Look, mate. Don't lie. I know you've got a ten of coconuts." Smitty raised an eyebrow at Liam under the beams of the lantern swaying overhead in their cabin.

"I do not, Smitty. I've got a *six* of coconuts. And a nine of skulls. Don't tell me I'm a liar."

"A nine of skulls, hm?" Smitty studied his cards, chuckling deviously as Liam realized he'd stepped right into Smitty's trap.

"That's not fair!" the younger boy cried. "No wonder no one else'll play cards with you. You're a scoundrel!"

"Not really." Smitty looked pleased. "Just the best Go Plunder player on board. Maybe in all the seven seas."

Scarlet, curled in a hammock off to the side, cleared her throat, hoping they'd quiet down so she could sulk in silence. They didn't notice. Liam, red to his ears now, looked like he was about to throw down his cards and quit. Jem looked on, studying their game. It was similar, he'd said, to one he played back home, but with different suits. He seemed to think his clubs, hearts, diamonds, and spades were more civilized than cutlasses, coconuts, seashells, and skulls. Scarlet thought his version sounded downright boring.

She threw them all another cutlass glare, but it

bounced off them harmlessly and went unnoticed. Then she harrumphed and turned onto her other side, making the hammock swing and the cabin beams creak.

This, she decided, was the worst day of her life. No, maybe the second-worst day. Yesterday, when she'd led them all to a blasted lukewarm slough rather than a boiling lake, had been worse. But still, abandoning Lucas on the Island of Smelly Wild Pigs hadn't exactly been a picnic. Only an hour ago, she'd felt the entire crew's eyes on her as Emmett and Edwin rowed Lucas to the island's shore under the dim light of a crescent moon. They were all waiting to see if she'd really go through with it and leave the boy to a possible death at the hooves of a pack of swine. As she watched the rowboat bounce over the waves, she felt like yelling for the boys to come back. But if she did, it would mean Lucas had won. No one would ever take her seriously as captain again—least of all, Lucas. On the other hand, Lucas's cronies would hate her even more for reducing their leader to wild pig bait. When he came back, she might even have a mutiny on her hands. Things would never be the same on board the *Margaret's Hop.*

It also spoiled their plan to return to Island X the following day. Stupid, stupid Lucas Lawrence.

Scarlet sighed. *What would Ben Hodgins have done in my place?* she wondered. *Would he have found an alternative punishment as he did the time Lucas hoarded spoils for himself? Or would he, too, have left his best carpenter on an island of vicious—*

"What's the story with these smelly wild pigs,

anyway?" As if on cue, Jem looked up from the card game to ask yet another question. *Boys have no tact,* Scarlet thought. Instead of answering, she grunted and flopped over again on the hammock.

Smitty and Liam, equally tactless, abandoned their game and dove right into the new topic.

"Well, first of all," said Liam, "they're about the smelliest animals in the entire world."

"What do they smell like?" Jem asked.

"Rubbish," said Liam.

"Sweaty feet," Smitty offered.

"Rotten flounder."

"The long drop after Liam's eaten too much guava fruit!" Smitty hooted, and Liam shook a small fist.

"All right, so they stink. But are they dangerous?" Jem asked.

"Are they dangerous?" Smitty said. "Try downright beastly. They hunt in packs, see? Twenty or thirty hogs to a group. And they move stealthily through the jungle, silent except for a rustle here and there." The lantern illuminated Smitty's eyes and made shadows dance on his face. "And then suddenly, when you least expect it, they're surrounding you. All of them, with big horse teeth and hooves they've sharpened on boulders in their spare time. And they rip you limb from limb! Tearing and piercing and—"

"Ahem." Liam elbowed Smitty and tilted his head toward Scarlet, who felt like she might spew and knew she looked it, too. Smitty closed his mouth.

"But sometimes they're not so bad," Liam hastened

to add. "Sometimes they just want to . . . um . . . play."

Scarlet groaned and tossed in the hammock.

Thankfully, Tim poked his head into the cabin and interrupted the discussion. "Glad I've found you all here," he said, sitting down on an old crate and peering at them over his spectacles. "I've been doing some reading."

"Reading?" Smitty said. "You? Sink me!"

"Shut up, Aloysius. I've been wondering all day why Lucas would risk punishment to steal Jem's knife. I wondered if maybe he knew something about it that we didn't."

"I assumed he just liked the look of it," Jem said.

"I assumed he was just being a big—"

"Well, you both might be right," Tim hurried on before Smitty could offer his theory. "But I thought I'd check it out. And look what I found." He laid a pile of old papers on his lap and thumbed through them until he found what he wanted. "Cutthroat MacPhee," he said. Scarlet sat up in the hammock at the mention of the knife's previous owner. "The most bloodthirsty pirate ever to sail these waters. Deadlier than Deadeye Johnny. More dreaded than the Dread Pirate Rosella. The pirate to end all pirates." Tim looked up from his papers and pulled off his spectacles. "Apparently, Cutthroat MacPhee ruled the seas. He and his crew always took the best plunder, the fastest ships, the tastiest rum. Every pirate wanted to be on his crew so they'd never have to be on the receiving end of his blade or his cannonballs. No one could defeat Cutthroat MacPhee, and he became a legend."

"So what happened to him?" Jem piped up.

Tim looked annoyed. "I'm getting to it, mate. See, even old Cutthroat had a weakness. He was terrified, just scared to death, of snakes. And, so the story goes, the islands knew it. Cutthroat was searching for treasure inland one day, and he got separated from his crew. They found him later, cold as the ocean's floor, lying among a great writhing mass of snakes. Hundreds of 'em, all snuggled up to the world's deadliest pirate. It didn't matter that they weren't poisonous. Cutthroat MacPhee died of fright."

Smitty shuddered. Liam chewed his lip. Jem cocked his head to one side.

"There's a term for a great writhing mass of snakes," he said. "My uncle told me once, but I can't remember it. Anyway, it's a good story, but how does it explain why my knife's so valuable?"

"Blimey, you ask lots of questions. The death of Cutthroat MacPhee did two things. It made the pirates even more scared of the islands, and it made their hero even more celebrated. Everything he owned, from his pocket watch to his false teeth, became treasures in the eyes of the pirates."

"His teeth?" Scarlet finally spoke up. "Who'd want a set of skuzzy old chompers?" She'd enjoyed the story, but it had done little to soothe her crusty mood.

"When I meet my end, pirates everywhere'll fight over my remains," Smitty said dreamily. "They'll keep my eyes in a jar near the ship's wheel, looking out over the water. 'Here sits the great pirate Saltwater Smith,' they'll say. And they'll all cross their hearts in respect."

"The great pirate Neville is more like it," Scarlet muttered. "So you think Lucas knew the value of Jem's knife, and the story behind it?"

"How would he know?" Liam asked.

"Well, he does seem to know a lot about grown-up pirates," Tim said.

Jem cleared his throat. "Um, he might know even more than you think." They all turned to him. "Remember when I stole the knife in Jamestown, and Lucas helped me escape from Deadeye Johnny and the others who wanted to kill me?" The other Lost Souls nodded. "Well, Lucas helped by convincing Deadeye that he hadn't seen me, and that if he did, he'd turn me in. They talked like old friends. I probably should have mentioned that sooner."

Scarlet and her friends looked at one another with identical expressions of unease.

"All right. So Lucas is friends with the deadliest pirate around. What does this mean for us?" Tim said.

"Nothing good." Smitty shook his head, looking grim. "Maybe we should just leave the sea dog on the island and forget about him."

It was all too much for Scarlet. She stood up. "I'm going to bed," she announced, although she knew that even sleep wouldn't help her state of mind. What she needed was something to keep her thoughts off Lucas and the smelly wild pigs for the next twenty-three hours. "Let's go to port tomorrow," she said. "We'll need food and supplies before we return to Island X." But even the thought of the treasure hunt didn't improve her mood.

"Right, Captain," Tim said. "Port Aberhard's no

more than a few hours' sail from here. We'll lay anchor at dawn and be back in plenty of time to pick up the scourge tomorrow night." He gave her a small smile. She tried to return it, tried to think of something captainly and motivating to say, but in the end she simply wandered out, thoughts tossing in her head like whitecaps on waves.

Scarlet wasn't sure what she was looking for in Port Aberhard. She drifted down the streets, skirting clusters of pirates and King's Men without noticing them. She scanned the merchants' tables and saw little of interest. But she pocketed a tarnished compass and two tins of herring for good measure. After meandering for about an hour, she realized that all the random supplies she could squeeze in her pockets weren't going to help her solve her problems.

Scarlet sighed. This was pointless. She'd do better heading back to the ship and concentrating on preparing for their trip to Island X the next morning. That was the most important thing, after—

"You're not serious, are you, man? That's an absurd price for a bag of spice. Why, it's harvested right here on the island."

Scarlet stopped dead. She knew that voice. She'd been missing it for too long now. Pivoting on her tiptoes, she scanned the scene until she found the voice's owner.

Ben Hodgins stood not ten yards away haggling with a spice merchant, but had she not heard his voice, Scarlet might not even have recognized him. Someone had chopped off his unruly brown hair, and now it hung perfectly combed and lifeless just above his earlobes. Ben's face looked unnaturally clean, making Scarlet wonder how much scrubbing it had taken to get that way. Then she wondered, for the first time ever, if she herself might need a bath.

She got her answer in the form of a young woman standing beside him—equally spotless, with ears that had likely never known a speck of dirt, let alone a small family of gnats. Scarlet pulled absently at her own earlobes, glad the bugs had evacuated after a few days. The girl had a cherubic face and soft, brown curls, and she watched Ben barter with a look of adoration. Scarlet felt her cheeks flush as she realized she'd worn that expression herself, many times.

For an instant she considered hollering a hello. But then she stopped herself. Ben was a grown-up now. He had a wife-to-be. Would he even want to acknowledge her?

Scarlet turned to slink off through the crowd, then stopped when she heard his voice again. "McCray! Wait!"

Suddenly he was beside her with one hand on her shoulder, turning her around to face him, his bright eyes (at least *they* still looked the same) looking into hers with the mischievous glee she remembered so well.

But it only lasted a moment before Ben dropped his hand and glanced back at the young woman, who was giving him a quizzical look. Both he and Scarlet took a step away from each other.

"Scarlet, how are you? I've missed, I mean . . . I can't believe how long it's been."

"I'm fine," Scarlet answered. "We're . . . we're all fine. The crew, that is." Awkward conversations, she decided, were just as bad as awkward silences. "How are you? You look . . . different."

Ben glanced at the girl again and waved as if to say "Be with you in a moment." Then he took Scarlet's arm and led her away, toward the docks. For a moment, Scarlet felt smug—Ben had left his future wife to walk with her—until she remembered her cabin boy disguise. The girl would have thought she was simply another scruffy boy.

"So?" Ben said once they'd walked a little. "What's new? Tell me everything."

Where to begin? Scarlet wondered. "Well, let's see. The *Hop*'s holding up well enough—should last us another year at least. And we've had some successful raids lately. Oh, and we've got a map to the treasure that everyone's looking for. We're heading out to find it tomorrow. I mean, we've been out once already, but, well, it's a bit of a long story. You see, the treasure's on one of *those* islands, and—"

But Ben was scanning the port, looking as if he'd left his brain on the spice merchant's table with the angel-faced girl. "That's nice," he muttered.

"All right then," Scarlet cut her story short. "What's new with you?"

"Hm? Oh, me? Well, you know. Domestic things. Respectable things. I'm learning to manage my future father-in-law's tobacco plantation now. It's a lot of work, but a lucrative business."

Scarlet raised an eyebrow at him. She'd never heard the Lost Souls's former captain use the words *respectable* and *lucrative* without following up with a joke.

"Oh, and we're—Cecily and I, that is—we're getting married next year. And now there's all this talk about having children right away, to, you know, ensure that there's a next generation to take over the plantation. Real children, Scarlet. Can you imagine?" His voice trembled ever so slightly.

Scarlet didn't know what to say. Ben Hodgins, soon to be a father. He suddenly seemed very far away although he stood right next to her.

"Congratulations," she said, hoping it didn't fall flat.

Ben turned to face her. "It's a scary thing, Scarlet. I thought being captain of the Lost Souls was frightening business. That has nothing on raising a child. See—"

"You found being captain frightening?" Scarlet cut in. That couldn't be. Ben's confidence had been practically contagious.

He nodded. "Sure. It's a tough job. But nothing, like I said—"

"Right, right, like being a father," Scarlet interrupted again. "But the crew always loved you. If you picked up a pan flute and danced off the plank, they would have followed, single file. You never even—"

"Scarlet." It was Ben's turn to interrupt. "What's wrong? Something's up, I can sense it." Finally, he was listening.

Scarlet lowered her eyes. She would have bared her

soul to the old Ben Hodgins. But this well-groomed version? She wasn't sure.

"Tell me."

She hesitated and scanned his face for a trace of her old friend. She found it in his eyes, the eyes that had welcomed her that first day, so long ago. The eyes she could never resist confiding in.

She confided again. She explained everything that had gone on in the past week as fast as she could but without leaving out any important details.

Once she'd gotten to the part about how they'd left Lucas on the Island of Smelly Wild Pigs, Ben was looking overwhelmed. Evidently not even the angst of impending fatherhood could compare to her situation.

"Sink me, Scarlet, I don't know what to say. That business with Lucas really scuttles. But I know you'll pull through. You're a good captain, and you'll figure it out."

And with that, he looked back toward the merchant's stall to check on his future wife.

Scarlet felt her cheeks flush. He couldn't even focus on her for more than a moment before returning to his own affairs. She pressed on. "Well, I'm not so sure of that. I don't even know if I'm captain material, to tell you the truth. I often wonder if I can ever live up to the great Ben Hodgins . . ."

She hadn't meant for that last bit to slip out. But it got Ben's full attention. He snapped his head away from the port and stared at her. And when he spoke, he sounded almost angry.

"Scarlet, what's the matter with you? You don't sound like the captain I appointed. 'The great Ben Hodgins'? That's bilge. A captain's only as good as his crew and you know it. I chose you because you're an essential part of the Lost Souls. But if you don't know that, and show it, how will the others know?"

"But . . . but," she sputtered, aware that she was sounding more and more childish the longer she persisted. "How can you be sure I'm the one to lead? I don't know what to do. Can't you give me some direction?"

"Benjamin! We have to go!"

"Coming!" Ben called back, in a deeper voice than the one with which he addressed Scarlet. She shook her head and started to turn away, but he stopped her with a hand on her arm.

"I chose you because you're one of the bravest people I've ever met. Remember when you saved me from the King's Man years ago? You don't run away from problems. You face them. And what's more, you care about the crew. They need that. Look, Scarlet, you have all the answers you need. You've just got to listen to the people around you and, more importantly, listen to yourself. All the answers you need are there."

He slapped her on the shoulder, like a fellow sailor. "Now go find that treasure." Then he marched back into port. To his future wife and his new life.

Scarlet watched his back for a minute, until it disappeared among a sea of other grown-ups. Then she turned and ran.

She said very little to Tim, Emmett, and Edwin as they rowed out to the Island of Smelly Wild Pigs. The sun had ducked behind the horizon, leaving the violet sky blotched with rosy-gray and streaks of peach. She'd considered staying on board the *Hop*, but decided at the last minute to accompany the boys and perhaps have a word with Lucas before they rejoined the rest of the crew. As the rowboat rose and fell with the waves, she wondered what she'd say. Declare a truce? Apologize for leaving him to be mauled by a pack of sweaty swine? Or tell him that if he were ever caught stealing again, the next punishment would make the pigs look downright sociable?

"I don't see him," Emmett said. Scarlet tore her eyes away from the clouds and looked toward the shore. The island's thin strip of beach looked empty. Beyond it, a wall of trees rose straight up from the sand. Lucas was nowhere to be seen.

Emmett and Edwin vaulted over the side of the boat and splashed through the shallows to the shore, calling Lucas's name. Only a creepy silence followed. Nothing moved, not even the wall of green that separated jungle and sea.

Scarlet's heart began to pound. *The pigs,* she thought. *The pigs must have gotten him. Oh, what was I thinking, leaving him on the island overnight?* Visions of horse teeth and sharpened hooves flooded her brain, and she gripped the side of the boat, certain now she was going to spew.

"Scarlet, stop. You're rocking the boat," Tim said. "He's probably hiding." But even her quartermaster looked concerned as the twins ran up and down the beach, shouting for Lucas. They ducked into the jungle for a quick look, disappearing behind the leafy curtain. Minutes passed. Scarlet still held the side of the boat, afraid she'd faint if she let go.

Tim wouldn't tear his gaze from the shore. "C'mon, Lucas," he muttered. "Stop being a scoundrel and come out."

But when the twins emerged, they were alone. They walked slowly down to the shoreline and into the shallow water.

"Well?" Scarlet managed to say.

Emmett shrugged. "No trace, Captain."

Edwin shook his head. "He's gone."

CHAPTER THIRTEEN

After envisioning all the worst possible ways Lucas could have met his end, from suffocating under the stench of wild pigs to falling headfirst out of a tree he'd climbed to escape the beasts, Scarlet somehow fell into an uneasy sleep. When she awoke the next morning, she decided to do something. She decided to take someone's advice.

You have all the answers you need, Ben had told her. *You've just got to listen. Listen to the people around you and, more importantly, listen to yourself. All the answers you need are there.*

And so, as perplexed as she was by her meeting with the new Ben Hodgins, she had to admit she had no better ideas. She would listen as hard as she could and hope for an answer to her most pressing question, "How the flotsam am I going to deal with this blasted situation?"

Listen inside and out. Scarlet squeezed her eyes shut and tried to listen. Beside her, tangled in her own hammock, little Ronagh muttered in her sleep. Something about a pet monkey that juggled daggers and played the trombone. Despite herself, Scarlet giggled. Not exactly the answer she was looking for.

She slipped out of her hammock, pushed her bare feet into her boots, noted a new hole under the left big toe, and crept out of the cabin. No one else was awake except a pair of pirates on lookout duty. Even the sun had yet to peek over the horizon, although the sky was growing pale in preparation.

Listen. She stood on the quarterdeck and closed her eyes again. She heard the slap of waves against the hull and the cry of two gulls overhead. The wind whooshing in her ears. A fish breaking through the water close by. But no answers.

Maybe they weren't going to make themselves heard so easily. Maybe she'd have to be quieter, stealthier, sneak up on them when they least expected it. The thought amused her, although she suspected that her lack of sleep was making it more amusing than it really was. Still, she decided to approach the task like a spy. She'd make herself scarce and listen all day.

The other Lost Souls began to emerge from their cabins just as the sun climbed over the horizon. They divvied up a few loaves of bread and some bananas stolen from port the previous day, then got down to their chores, quieter than usual. No one mentioned Lucas, but he was clearly on everyone's mind.

Scarlet heard the first rumors while rounding a corner on the cabin deck, mid-morning. At the sound of hushed voices, she flattened herself against the wall and peeked around it, spying two boys whispering as they untangled fishing nets.

"They say the pigs got him, but I think he's hiding," said Elmo. "That'd be just like old Lucas, trying to get revenge by scaring us."

"Shh," Monty hissed, glancing around. "I heard Lucas went mad with fright that night and joined up with a band of monkeys. He's out there now, swinging in the treetops."

"That's bilge!" Elmo exclaimed, then lowered his voice. "How would anyone know that?"

"I heard it from Stephen who heard it from Ronagh who heard it from Emmett, and Emmett was on the island searching for Lucas last night, so he'd know better than anyone."

Monty shrugged. "Could happen."

"Could not. Lucas is too big to swing in treetops. The branches would break."

Scarlet rolled her eyes and moved away. Of course it was ridiculous—Lucas, captain of a posse of monkeys? Fitting perhaps, but complete bilge. Still, if rumors were already making the rounds, they'd probably grow more far-fetched by the hour.

She was sneaking past Lucas's own cabin when her ears—now in full spy mode—picked up another intriguing conversation. This time one of the voices belonged to Gil Jenkins; she could tell even before she peeked into the room and saw the boy standing beside Lucas's hammock with Sam and Charlie. Gil, looking regretful, held an old dagger that had lost its handle.

"This was his first weapon," Gil told the others. "But it's mine now, since I was closest to him."

"Gil, you don't know he's dead for sure," Charlie pointed out.

Gil shrugged and touched the dull blade. "But it's most likely. Even Lucas couldn't survive a pack of smelly wild pigs." He bowed his head. "He would've made a good captain. Now there's no way we can mutiny. Too bad. Would've been good fun."

From her hiding place on the other side of the doorway, Scarlet gasped. So they *had* been planning to mutiny. Those rotten little stinkers. She edged closer to the door, imagining the looks on their faces if she leaped into the room and caught them in this act of treason. What was the punishment for treason, anyway? Maybe a good old-fashioned keelhaul, a torture reserved for only the nastiest offenders. It involved binding a traitor's hands to a rope that passed underneath the ship, from bow to stern. He'd be thrown overboard, and the pirates on board would pull him back and forth under the vessel, like a human careening tool. Scarlet could practically taste the satisfaction she'd feel watching horrible little Gil Jenkins sputtering in the dark waters, begging for mercy.

Sam wiped his nose with his sleeve. "He was a strong pirate," he said as if he'd come to Lucas's empty hammock to pay his last respects.

"He probably would've led us to the treasure," Charlie added. The boys fell silent for a minute, then looked at one another and shrugged as if they'd run out of respectful things to say. Even Scarlet couldn't think of anything else to add. Strong and driven by the promise of the legendary treasure summed Lucas up pretty well.

The boys abandoned their eulogy and made ready to leave. Scarlet scurried back down the hallway and up the stairs to the main deck where she busied herself studying cracks in the floorboards. This listening-for-answers strategy had only resulted in a dozen more questions—like, for instance: Would Lucas really have made a good leader? A better leader than her? She tried to picture him as captain and decided that while he might keep their pockets full of pieces of eight (well, his own pockets, anyway), life under Lucas's command would scuttle.

Lucas simply wasn't a true Lost Soul. The Lost Souls' way of life had never been good enough for him, and he'd even gone against one of their core beliefs to hoard bounty for himself. Lucas didn't care about the crew. He only wanted the pillagings. Scarlet, on the other hand, cared fiercely about the Lost Souls. She *wanted* to lead them, and she wanted to do it well.

She stopped and looked out at the ocean. The sun shimmered on its surface as if fireworks were exploding just underneath. As she watched the sea, her ears picked up one last important sound, an almost foreign noise. It was the sound of silence on deck. Her crew was going about their chores without songs or jokes or banter, each on his or her own.

Scarlet chewed her lip. This would never do. The *Margaret's Hop* was supposed to be a jolly home for children throughout the islands, and the Lost Souls counted on Scarlet to make it so. They also looked to her to fulfill their mission and lead them to the treasure.

It was time to make good on her promises.

"All good pirates, come to order!"

Scarlet stood on the poop deck near the wheel, looking down on her crew. She planted her boots firmly on the deck, swept her hair off her face, and set her fists on her hips. The crew looked back at her expectantly, and she saw a few glances pass between Lucas's allies. *Be strong,* she told herself. *Be Captain.*

"I'm sure you're all wondering why we dropped anchor for this meeting," she began in her best captain voice. More glances passed, along with a few shrugs. "Well, you see, it's . . ." Scarlet stopped. This wasn't right. She sat down on the poop deck, swinging her legs out over the edge toward them. The Lost Souls clustered closer.

"All right. First I want to . . . apologize." It was one of the hardest words she'd ever had to spit out. A few murmurs and eyebrows rose before her. "Of course I'm talking about Lucas. I didn't mean for this to happen, and I'm no less upset than any of you that he's disappeared. He broke an important rule, yes, but he didn't deserve to . . . you know . . . if indeed he is . . ." Scarlet found that she couldn't even say it. "Anyway, it's made me think about my position as captain, as I know some of you have been doing, too." Here she looked directly at Gil Jenkins, who flushed and folded his arms over his chest. Behind him, Jem was studying the floorboards with an intensity that told Scarlet he'd known about Lucas's plan. *Would he have joined the mutiny?* she wondered, then dismissed the thought. Jem Fitzgerald was too good for that.

Scarlet shook her head and continued. "From now on, if there's a problem with the way things are run on board, I want you to tell *me*. Not your cabinmate. Me." She surveyed Lucas's followers, letting her eyes linger on Gil for a long moment. He opened his mouth as if to speak, then seemed to think better of it and shut it. Neither Charlie nor Sam made a sound. This didn't surprise Scarlet; without Lucas to lead them, the rebels were practically powerless.

All the same, she still wouldn't have minded keelhauling their sorry rear ends.

"I want you all to know that I'm not giving up on Lucas," she said. "We'll head back to the Island of Smelly Wild Pigs first thing tomorrow for another look around. We'll look for clues and hopefully find some answers."

A few crew members nodded. Gil looked a little nervous, probably because he'd already claimed some of Lucas's belongings.

"We're also not giving up on the treasure," she added. "Our first attempt failed, but we'll learn from it and try again." She looked at Jem, who looked up from the floorboards and nodded. "I made a promise, and I'm not going back on it.

"But now, before heading back to Island X, there's something we have to do." She hoped they'd be up for this next part. "This is an important step in finding the treasure. Plus, it could be fun." She hopped off the deck and stood among them. "Tonight, we're going to get suited up for a raid."

"A raid?" one pirate exclaimed.

"Yesss!" Ronagh punched the air.

A few others exchanged crafty grins and began to whisper among themselves.

"I'll have to mend my cloak!" one cried.

"I've been practicing some new ghostly noises,"

another pirate said excitedly. "Wanna hear?"

Scarlet smiled. Nothing brought the Lost Souls together like a ship raid.

"So what are we raiding for?" Emmett and Edwin chorused.

"Seriously," Emmett added, "what's the purpose of the raid?"

"Who cares?" Smitty yelled. "It's a raid, mates. Let's go."

"Actually, there is a purpose. Three purposes, really. One: to scare the pants off some deserving pirates. Two: to steal the usual food and supplies. Three: to get some answers. From the *Dark Ranger* pirates."

Someone gasped. "We're raiding the *Dark Ranger* again?"

Scarlet scanned the crowd until she found the horror-stricken face she was looking for. "Don't you worry, Fitz," she said. "You can trust me."

CHAPTER FOURTEEN

"You look fantastic, Fitz."

"I can't believe we're doing this."

"If only you could see yourself. You're high fashion in the world of ghosts and ghouls."

"Raiding the *Dark Ranger*? Scarlet, are you out of your mind?"

"Look out, afterworld—here comes Fitz! C'mon, let's see your most ghoulish strut."

"You're mad."

She was madder than mad. Scarlet McCray was absolutely insane if she thought he was going to set foot on that ship again. Jem didn't care how many layers of black cloth disguised him. He'd been lucky to escape Captain Wallace and his crew once; no way was he going to chance it again. No way. He folded his arms across his chest.

"Now, Fitz. It makes all the sense in the world," Scarlet pleaded as she pinned up the hem of his cloak so he wouldn't trip when he walked. (This, of course, only emphasized his being short and made him even less willing to cooperate.) "We know that the so-called Dread Pirate Hammerstein Captain Jones Wallace—or whatever his name is—is ridiculously afraid of us, and so is the rest of his crew. So we'll hop on board, scare the trousers off 'em, search for some clues as to your uncle's whereabouts, then leave. Oh, and maybe pinch a tin of herring or two. And some preserves if they have any."

Jem stared at Scarlet, wondering if this whole Smelly Wild Pig fiasco had somehow altered her ability to think straight. She honestly seemed to believe that he'd benefit from this raid, that hopping onto the *Dark Ranger* might actually prove that his uncle was still alive. It was a nice thought, and one he wished he could believe in, but it didn't seem possible. Scarlet seemed to have overlooked the fact that if Captain Wallace and his crew got their hands on him this time, he'd be shark bait. No doubt about it.

Smitty gave a whistle of admiration as he strolled through the cabin door, carrying his own cloak. "Nice outfit, Fitz." Tim, Liam, and Ronagh followed, each with an armload of black cloth. They'd smeared coal dust all over their faces so only the whites of their eyes and their bared teeth would stand out against their cloaks.

"It suits you," Liam commented, giving Jem a once-over.

"Brings out your eyes." Ronagh laughed and batted her eyelashes at him.

"See?" Scarlet stood up to survey her hemming work. "I told you." She turned to her friends. "Fitz here is scared he'll get discovered even with the disguise. What d'you think?"

Smitty and Liam shook their heads.

"It's never happened. Pirates everywhere fear the Ship of Lost Souls," said Tim. "The legend has been around too long, and we appear often enough to keep them from forgetting it. Anyway, your cloak's big enough to hide a cutlass underneath in case anything goes wrong. I'll see if we have a spare for you."

Jem gulped. He'd never wielded any weapon larger than his pocketknife, and even then it had only been to butter his bread.

"Now, Scarlet," Tim said. "What's going on with Gil Jenkins and Lucas's little band of sheep? What were you talking about when you said some sailors have been questioning you as captain?"

Scarlet crouched to adjust Jem's hem. "There was a plan to mutiny," she murmured through the pins she held between her lips.

"Mutiny?" Ronagh screeched.

"What? Those little swabs! I'd like to see them try!" Smitty put one hand on the hilt of his cutlass.

Jem tried to look surprised at the news. He wondered how long Scarlet had known, and if she also knew that Lucas had asked him to join.

"Surely you aren't taking it to heart, though," Tim said. "I mean, they're just a few troublemakers who need their ears boxed."

Scarlet shrugged and drove a pin through Jem's cloak.

Jem highly doubted that, if it came right down to it, anyone would actually mutiny against Captain McCray. But he didn't offer his opinion aloud. Since he'd been on board for only a few days, his observations probably wouldn't count for much. Plus, he had bigger, more pressing things to dwell on at the moment. Like the completely illogical plan to hop onto the ship of the pirates who'd kidnapped him and killed his uncle. And the nausea growing in his gut.

"Let's not talk about it now. We've got a big raid ahead of us, and I want to make sure we're organized so it goes smoothly," Scarlet said. She took the pins out of her mouth and motioned for them all to sit down. They formed a circle, cross-legged, on the cabin floor. "There'll be three parts to this raid, so I want to divide us into three teams. First, we'll have a stealing crew made up of our best pillagers and led by none other than Quickfingers Smith."

"At your service, Cap'n."

"Then there'll be a scaring team, which I'll lead. Liam and Ronagh, you'll come with me. We'll terrorize the pirates until they tell us what we want to hear.

"Last, we have our searching team. Jem will lead that crew, and Swig, you'll go, too. You'll sneak around looking for clues as to your uncle's whereabouts. Steal and scare if you must, but concentrate on the clues. Sound good?"

"Jolly!" the other pirates chorused. But Jem, though flattered that he'd been made captain of his very own team, could only muster a halfhearted "Great."

"Come on, Fitz. We could do this with our eyes closed," Smitty said. "Trust us. No one will ever recognize you. No way."

"Steady now, Smitty. Sure you can do this?"

Smitty paused, grappling iron and rope in hand, and

shot Tim an irritated look. "Course I can do this, Swig. All it takes is a little aim."

Tim shrugged and stepped back beside Jem and Scarlet. They stood on the quarterdeck with all the other Lost Souls, dressed in black, faces coated with charcoal. Beside and above them, the *Dark Ranger* loomed against the midnight sky. It felt like just yesterday that Jem had escaped this very schooner. He still couldn't believe he was willingly going to climb on again. This was so far beyond logic it made his head spin.

Smitty squinted, lifted the grappling iron again, and prepared to hurl it over the *Dark Ranger*'s edge so they could get on board by climbing the rope attached to it.

"He's never done this before?" Jem whispered to Scarlet as everyone watched Smitty take a few practice swings.

Scarlet shook her head, and her forehead wrinkled under a layer of coal dust. "Lucas always did it. He was the strongest and had the best aim."

"I heard that," Smitty called out. "And I'll have you know I'm just as strong and just as—"

"Shut up, Smit," Tim hissed. "Do it quick, before they spot us."

"All right, all right." With a grunt, Smitty wound up and launched the grappling iron toward the schooner's side. The Lost Souls held their breath and watched the iron arcing through the air, illuminated by the moonlight. For a moment, it looked like it wouldn't quite clear the ship's edge, but it did, just barely, and anchored to the wood with a satisfying crack.

"Told you," Smitty said. Scarlet patted him on the back.

"Jolly. All right, pirates, gather round. Quickly now. We'll only have a moment before they notice the rope, and we want to be on board before they try to cut it." All the Lost Souls, even Gil Jenkins, who'd previously taken orders only from Lucas, huddled around her. She placed a fist into the center of their circle, and one by one, they all wriggled their arms out of their cloaks to place their fists on top. Jem eyed the tower of hands. He could still refuse to go with them. Maybe he could guard the *Margaret's Hop*. That sounded like an important job. Maybe . . .

But they were all looking at him. Waiting. Jem sighed and settled his fist on top of the others.

"No prey, no pay, mateys," Scarlet said solemnly.

"No prey, no pay," the others chorused.

"Go smartly now, and may you die peacefully in your hammocks rather than keelhauled under the belly of a ship."

"Die peacefully!"

"Come on. Let's go!"

Scarlet grabbed the rope and scaled it effortlessly, with Smitty and Tim close behind. When it was his turn, Jem peered down at the black water, knowing he'd end up in it if he slipped during the climb. He swallowed, gripped the rope, and began to pull himself up, walking his feet up the side of the *Dark Ranger* as he put one hand over the other. After a few moments, he settled into the drill. It reminded him of the climbing ropes in the

King's Cross gymnasium, which in turn reminded him of his sensible schoolmaster. Master Davis would have never gone on such a mission.

But what about Uncle Finn? Jem wondered. If there were even the tiniest chance that Jem were still alive and being held captive on board the *Dark Ranger*, would Uncle Finn raid the ship to find him? Jem pictured his uncle slogging through waist-deep mud filled with venomous snakes and persistent leeches as he had in one of his adventures. Yes, Jem decided, Uncle Finn would face this danger.

Just as he was clambering over the schooner's edge and onto its main deck, a cry severed the silence and his thoughts.

"Invaders! We're under attack, mates!" A hefty, bearded pirate ran toward them from the fo'c'sle, holding a lantern in one hand and waving a broadsword with the other as if it weighed no more than a twig. A few others, equally gritty-looking, tromped out behind him. Smitty grabbed Jem by the arm and dragged him over the edge onto the deck. "Stand your ground," he said. "We've got to guard the rope until everyone's on board."

Hands trembling, Jem reached inside his trouser pocket for his knife. Tim never had found him a spare cutlass, which was just as well, because Jem couldn't actually see himself using one. He took his place beside Scarlet and Tim to face the pirates, wondering if this would be how he'd meet his end. But when the pirates drew near enough to recognize the Lost Souls, they all froze. One let out a noise that sounded more like the cry of a small child than a crusty pirate. "They're back," he wailed. "It's the Lost Souls!"

"Let's get 'em!" Tim whispered. "Smitty, stay here and make sure the others get up safely. Jem, come on! You'll love this!" And he bounded off after the pirates. Scarlet took off, too, and Jem had no choice but to follow. They circled the pirates, whose eyes were as big as doubloons, and backed them up against the mainmast. Cackling demonically, Tim and Scarlet began to skip around them in a kind of devilish maypole dance. Jem watched for a moment, unsure whether he could pull it off, but grew more confident the harder the pirates trembled. These sea dogs killed Uncle Finn, Jem reminded himself. Make them pay. And with that he launched himself into the dance, swerving in and out of the pirates' faces, throwing in a few spooky moans to terrify them even more.

More pirates soon arrived on the scene, along with more Lost Souls itching for action. Cries of "Not again!" and "This time they'll kill us all!" were answered by hoots and ghostly moans as the Lost Souls scattered across the deck, skipping and scampering and wreaking general havoc.

"Split up now!" Scarlet hissed after a few minutes. "Searchers down below. Stealers to the stern. Scarers, stay here with me!"

Breathless, Jem remembered his task. He wasn't about to get his hopes up about finding Uncle Finn, but he'd come this far and had to look around. He took off toward the staircase. But as he flung himself full tilt down the stairs, he ran smack into a massive figure.

"Argh!" the pirate yelled, and Jem immediately recognized his voice. It was Thomas, the gigantic softie. The big man backpedalled as fast as he could, half falling down the stairs and back down the hallway to the cabins, yelling, "They're back! The Lost Souls! Cap'n, they're back!"

Jem paused and shook his head. This was amazing. A bunch of pirate children who could barely lift their cutlasses, let alone use them as weapons, could actually terrify these bloodthirsty pirates.

"Fantastic, isn't it?" said the next ghoul over. It sounded like Emmett.

Another ghoul sighed. "It's a beautiful thing." Edwin, probably.

"All right, on with it. Let's find some clues." That was Tim for sure. They ran down the rest of the stairs and burst through the first door they saw.

It was a sleeping quarter, crisscrossed with hammocks and reeking of sweaty feet and morning breath. Edwin dove in, gagged at the smell, then ran back out. All the hammocks looked empty, and Jem shut the door as fast as he could.

"Scurvy, that stinks. I hope all the rooms aren't like that."

They found the next door on their right locked, but it shifted on its hinges, and when the boys threw all their weight against it, it gave way without much fuss. They tumbled into the room to find two men hunched over a chest full of pieces of eight. The men turned in surprise, and Jem found himself once again face-to-face with the

179

Dread Pirate Captain Wallace Hammerstein-Jones and his right-hand man, Iron "Pete" Morgan.

Forgetting his disguise, Jem ducked behind Emmett, remembering the captain screaming "Plank! Plank!" condemning Uncle Finn to death.

"Stand your ground," Emmett whispered, taking a few steps toward the pirates. Jem gulped and shuffled after him. Captain Wallace and Pete stared up at them, transfixed, as they slowly backed away on their hands and knees. The terror on their faces eased Jem's nerves, and as he reminded himself what these two had done to his uncle, his unease gave way to anger.

"P-p-p-please," the captain said, crawling backward until he hit the wall. He wiped his rodent nose and squinted at the Lost Souls. "Don't hurt us. Take a doubloon or two. Oh heck, take a sack of them. A small sack, mind you. And leave the shiny ones, please. Oh, and don't touch the rubies. I'm partial to rubies—"

"Captain." Pete shot his leader an incredulous look. "Captain, shut up!"

"Don't you tell me to shut up. I know how to handle this."

"Captain, you're trying to reason"—Pete threw his arms up in the air—"with the dead!"

"Oh, and I suppose you have a better idea?"

"Well, actually—"

"Ahem." Tim cleared his throat, and the pirates looked up as if they'd suddenly remembered the four ghouls standing before them. Jem rolled his eyes.

"Look, let me try," Pete said. He turned to the boys.

"Just listen for a moment. We're good pirates. We follow the laws of the sea. If we've offended you in some way, we're very sorry. Won't happen again."

Suddenly Captain Wallace jumped to his feet, hand on the cutlass at his hip. "That's it!" he cried, and jerked his weapon out of its sheath. Its blade glimmered in the low light. "I've had enough of this. If I'm going to die at the hands of the Lost Souls, I'm going to die fighting! Make sure they bronze my boots, Pete!"

And with that, he rushed toward the Lost Souls, his blade aimed right at Jem's nose. Jem ducked and dove out of the way, heart pounding, and the others spread out across the room. Pete scrambled to his feet and drew his weapon, too, looking less enthused at the prospect of dying a martyr.

Captain Wallace bounced off the wall and spun to face them again. Jem reached into his pocket and drew out his knife without tearing his eyes away from the captain's twitching lip. With a great "Argh!" the pirate charged once more, straight for him. But just as Captain Wallace was bounding across the cabin, a foot reached out and connected with his shin. The pirate turned a double-somersault and landed in a heap at Jem's feet. His cutlass spun across the floor, and Jem ran after it, snatching it up before Pete could. Then he turned toward the door to see the scaring team pouring in and surrounding the pirates. He had no doubt it had been Scarlet who tripped the captain.

Her whispers soon emanated from a cloak beside him. "Great work, Fitz. We'll take over now. Keep searching for clues."

Sopping with sweat under his cloak, Jem grasped his new weapon and started for the door, flanked by Tim and the twins. Outside the cabin, the four stopped and burst out laughing.

"Did you see their faces?" Tim cried.

Emmett mimicked Captain Wallace's moment of truth, brandishing an imaginary cutlass. "Bronze my stinky boots, Pete!" They doubled over, gasping for breath.

"All right," Jem said, finally regaining his composure. "Let's go on. We still have some searching to do."

Together, they continued down the hall. The next two rooms were sleeping quarters, equally smelly as the first, with no sign of Uncle Finn or any of his belongings. They had only one more room to search, at the very end of the hall. Jem shoved its door open, stepped inside, and froze.

"What d'ya see, Jem?"

"Is it your uncle?"

It was not Uncle Finn, no. Jem wouldn't have been quite so surprised to find his uncle mending sails on the *Dark Ranger* as he was to find Lucas Lawrence.

CHAPTER FIFTEEN

Lucas Lawrence lowered his needle and thread slowly and with a sly half smile that made Jem's fingers tremble as they closed around the hilt of Captain Wallace's cutlass underneath his cloak.

"Visitors." Lucas rose to his feet. "What a pleasant surprise."

The Lost Souls looked at one another, eight bewildered eyes peering out from black hoods.

"Lucas," Tim finally managed to squeak. "What are you doing here?"

"Wouldn't you love to know?" Lucas smirked. "But I think you'll just have to wait and see. For now, I'd get off this ship if I were you." He cast a scornful glance at their disguises. "Those aren't going to protect you forever. Not from *real* pirates."

Jem was grateful for the hood that hid his open mouth. He had no idea how Lucas had gotten there or what on earth the boy was doing mending the *Dark Ranger*'s sails. But he did know one thing: If the other pirates still believed in the curse of the Lost Souls—and it seemed, judging from their reactions on deck, that they did—they wouldn't be so easily fooled for long, not with Lucas around to set them straight. Jem also knew from the look in the boy's eyes that there was no sense hanging around to reason with him. It was a satisfied look, a look that said everything was going according to plan.

"Let's go." Jem spun on his heel and marched back out the cabin door, followed closely by his three teammates. They stomped side by side down the hallway without a word, but Jem could feel the confusion and fear hanging over them. He swung into the cabin where they'd left Scarlet to torture Pete Morgan and Captain Wallace.

She and her crew had been busy. The pirates' hands and feet were bound with scraps of cloth that looked like they'd been ripped off Captain Wallace's now-raggedy trouser legs. The captives sat back-to-back in the center of the room as the Lost Souls, daggers and cutlasses drawn, marched around them in a circle shrieking, "Give us our man, give us our man." The captain, who'd been declaring his intention to die a hero the last time Jem saw him, was now blubbering like a baby.

Jem stepped right into the middle of the circle and grabbed the sleeve of the ghoul whose shrieks sounded most like Scarlet. "We've got to get out of here," he whispered. "It's Lucas. He's here. He's joined the *Dark Ranger* pirates."

Scarlet froze. For a moment, she said nothing. Then, from the depths of her hood came the nastiest curse Jem had ever heard—so nasty, in fact, that it made both Captain Wallace and Pete Morgan blush and look down at their boots. Scarlet broke away from the circle and swept out the door, leaving Captain Wallace and Pete Morgan tied up on the floor and looking bewildered.

"Where? Where is he?" Her voice sounded strangled. Jem pointed, then hurried behind while Scarlet charged down the hall toward the last door. "Lucas!" she yelled, throwing herself across the threshold and right onto the boy's worktable where she proceeded to lunge for Lucas's throat. "What the flotsam do you think you're doing? Answer me! This is what you do, after all the Lost Souls have given you?" She released his neck and began to pound his chest with her fists. "How could you?"

"Pull her off," said Tim, who had appeared beside Jem. Together they grabbed Scarlet's arms and pulled her back. Lucas looked a little surprised, but all in all unfazed by Scarlet's wrath. He almost looked like he wanted to laugh, and Jem prayed he wouldn't; that would send Scarlet over the edge and straight for her cutlass for sure.

"Captain, stop," Jem said to her. "It'll do no good. We've got to get off this ship."

"That's right," Lucas spoke up, straightening his collar. "Listen to little Fitz and get your sorry selves off my ship. Or you'll pay for it, mark my words." Then he smiled with all his yellow teeth. "Actually, you're going to pay for it, anyway."

Scarlet stopped struggling at that point. Her fists fell to her sides. "Swig, gather the crew. Let's go."

"What's going on?" some of the Lost Souls murmured as they climbed the stairs back to the main deck. "Someone tell us what's up." But they had to wait until the stealers had been alerted and herded back to the grappling iron, and all three teams had slid back down the rope onto the *Hop* before they found out the reason behind the hasty retreat.

"Lucas Lawrence?" Ronagh screeched when she heard.

"That scurvy swine! That scourge of the seven seas!" Smitty slashed the rope that connected the two ships as if he wished it were Lucas's right arm.

Jem looked up at the *Dark Ranger* as the *Margaret's Hop* began to pull away. Captain Wallace peered over the edge at them, lips twitching into a slow smile. "Ha!" the captain yelled, then turned back to his crew. "I scared off the Lost Souls! Did you all see that? The Lost Souls cowered at the very sight of me!"

Well, Jem thought, it seemed that Lucas hadn't gone and revealed their identity just yet. But it was only a matter of time.

A few Lost Souls scurried about tending to the sails, but most stayed to watch Scarlet pace the main deck, muttering, "What does it mean? What does it mean?" Then she stopped and scanned the crew. "Gil Jenkins! Where is he?" she bellowed.

Smitty plunged into the crowd and emerged, after a brief scuffle, with a squirming Gil Jenkins, who'd been a stealer during the raid. Someone produced a chair, and Smitty shoved the boy down onto it.

"Ow!" Gil protested. "Why me?"

"Should I tie 'im up?" Smitty asked Scarlet, who regarded Gil as if he were a shark circling the ship.

"Yes. Get the thickest, itchiest rope you can find." To Gil she said, "I've got some questions for you, and you'd better be ready to answer."

"Right," Smitty chimed in, "like what do you know about this?"

"And how did this happen?" Tim hollered from his

place behind the ship's wheel, steering them through the black night.

"And what does this *mean*?" Scarlet bellowed.

"All right." Jem stepped forward, hoping he could help by keeping a logical, cool head. "Everyone calm down. One question at a time."

"Right." Scarlet took a deep breath. "Gil, you might be Lucas's friend, but you're also a Lost Soul. You must tell us what you know. First off, how would the pirates have found Lucas on the island?"

Gil grunted and shrugged. Smitty whipped his dagger out of his boot and pointed it between the boy's eyes.

"All right, all right. I'm guessing that since Lucas went to the trouble of learning all about the other pirate ships over the years, he used some kind of code or smoke signal to attract their attention." Gil shrugged again. "But since I wasn't there, how would I know?" He crossed his arms and leaned back in his chair.

The answer made sense to Jem, who recalled Lucas's friendly exchange with Deadeye Johnny a few days earlier.

Scarlet drew another deep breath, evidently trying to keep a cool head herself. "All right then," she said through clenched teeth. "So Lucas decided he'd rather be a Dark Ranger than a Lost Soul. The next question is, what about our identity? Will he tell his new crew who we really are?"

"Of course he will," Smitty moaned. "He wants to see us fail, and he knows his new crew'll thank him nicely for telling our secret."

"He didn't even take the oath when he left!" Monty whispered.

"That's it. We're doomed!" Emmett wailed.

"We'll never fool anyone now," Edwin added.

"Wait a minute," Ronagh called out, and twenty-two heads turned to her. "Do you think Lucas'll take the pirates to the treasure?"

Twenty-two heads swiveled back to Gil, who was studying the calluses on his big toes.

"He couldn't," Smitty said. "He doesn't have a map."

"Would he need one? He might be able to remember the directions," Tim said.

"Um . . . ," Gil said to his calluses. He tugged at his collar as if it were a noose.

"Um *what*?" Scarlet's voice held daggers.

"Um . . . Lucas . . . um . . . might have, maybe . . . oh, scurvy. He's got the map."

"What?" Jem had to grab Scarlet's arms so that she wouldn't throw herself on Gil and wring his neck before he could explain. "What do you mean he has the map? When did he take it?"

"When he stole Jem's knife." Gil's voice was quiet now.

The announcement hit Jem like a blow to the head. He hadn't thought to check on the map since they'd returned from Island X.

"Who . . . who knew about this?" Scarlet wrenched herself out of Jem's grasp and turned to the rest of her crew. "WHO KNEW?"

No one answered, no hands were raised.

"Lucas only told me," Gil said. "Look, I'm not happy about this, either. When Lucas stole the map, he said that when we mutinied, I could expect a big slice of the booty. And now I won't see a speck of it."

Jem caught Scarlet's arms again before they could wrestle Gil into a headlock. He almost didn't, though, tempted to let the little traitor pay.

"What are we going to do?" Ronagh asked, her voice barely louder than a whisper.

Jem looked around at a sea of dejected charcoal-coated faces. Within a few minutes they'd gone from lively pirates to, well, lost souls. He could tell they were seconds away from giving up completely.

"We're going to go. To the treasure. Right now." As soon as the words escaped his mouth, Jem wondered where they'd come from. But he didn't take them back.

"Fitz, are you crazy?" Edwin said. "Lucas has our map *and* a gang of grown-up pirates on his side. We can't compete with that."

"Wait," Scarlet spoke up, wriggling out of Jem's hold. She looked at him as if he'd just invented a long drop that cleaned itself. "Jem's right. We're going, anyway. We've got to."

"But we've got no map!" someone yelled.

"Then we'll try to remember the way," Scarlet shot back.

"Their ship's faster than ours!" another pirate protested.

"If we get a head start, we might beat them," Scarlet said.

"They're bigger than us!" Ronagh said.

"We're smarter," Jem returned, and a few Lost Souls dared to giggle.

Scarlet nodded. "By the time the pirates reach Island X, we'll be waiting onshore to scare them off."

The pirates began to murmur among themselves. "But how?" one asked. "What if Lucas has already told them we're only children? They won't be scared of us."

Scarlet paused for a moment. "Then it's time for us to be real pirates," she said. "It's time for us to show them, and ourselves, that we're more than just children."

"We are?" Ronagh had to ask.

"What do you mean, 'We are?' We can pillage with the best of 'em. Swig could sail blindfolded in the fog, and Liam's sneer'll make your heart stop. We've got a ship that's never let us down. I'd say we're some of the best pirates around, of any age, and it's time we face these old sea swabs and conquer them."

The murmurs grew louder, and the crowd of Lost Souls began to wiggle and sway. Jem felt their energy swelling, and he decided that now would be the perfect time to prove their faith in their captain.

"All right then," he said. "Let's put it to a vote. All who want to stand behind Captain McCray and prove that children can be pirates, too, raise your hands."

Scarlet shot him a look of panic, but it was too late. Her status as captain had been challenged outright. Again.

The first hands in the air belonged to Smitty, Tim, Ronagh, Liam, and of course Jem. Then a few other hands shot up out of their cloaks. Followed by a few more. The night sky was already full of quivering fingers when Gil stood up to add his to the scene. His friends, seeing this, quickly added theirs.

Jem counted twenty-two hands, including his own. "Right then." Relieved, he gave Scarlet a grin. Then he yelled, in his most piratelike voice, "To Island X! Full speed ahead!"

CHAPTER SIXTEEN

This time, we're gold.
This time, we know.
This time we mean business.
Come on, let's go.
We're off to find the treasure
And give it its rightful home.

The pirates might be
Close behind,
But we are determined
That we will find
Our precious mys'try treasure
And give it its rightful home.

To Island X,
Full sail, top speed,
Without even looking
behind, 'cause we
won't leave without our treasure—

"Um, Smitty," Jem interrupted Smitty's latest impromptu chantey. "I think you'd better scrap that last verse."

Smitty stopped and gave Jem an irritated look. "If you think you can do better, mate—"

"No, no. It's just that I think we might . . . well . . . maybe we *should* look behind us." He frowned at something beyond the poop deck.

Scarlet and Tim squinted in that direction from their position at the wheel. Something had appeared on the horizon where the darkness was giving way to a pale dawn.

"It's a ship," Tim commented.

"Really? I thought it was a sea monster," Scarlet snapped. "Sorry," she added quickly, trying to remain gracious under pressure. "But that's not just any old ship." She shivered. They'd started out for Island X a few hours ago, not long after their getaway from the *Dark Ranger*. If Lucas had wasted no time in explaining the situation to Captain Wallace, and if his new crew had set out after the treasure right away, then that speck on the horizon was, in all likelihood, the *Dark Ranger*. And that truly scuttled.

She didn't have to say any of this out loud to her friends. They understood. "But how can we be sure it's them?" Jem asked. He'd shed his black cloak but hadn't bothered to wipe the coal dust off his face. No one had. They had more important things to do.

Smitty wriggled his eyebrows. "Just so happens I can help with that," he said. "Take a look at what your uncle Quickfingers pinched from the *Dark Ranger*." He disappeared down the stairs to the cabins, then reemerged moments later carrying a cylindrical leather case. Smitty tipped open the case. Out slid a shiny gold tube.

"A spyglass!" Tim cried. "And a fancy one, at that. Smitty, where'd you find this?"

Smitty shrugged. "In the captain's quarters."

Jem reached out and nabbed the spyglass from Smitty's quick fingers. He looked at it the same way one might look at a lost spaniel that found its way home.

"It's my uncle's," he said quietly.

Scarlet didn't know what to say. Their raid had failed to turn up any sign of Uncle Finn. She hadn't even had enough time to convince Captain Wallace to stop blubbering and tell her about the man's whereabouts before the searchers' unpleasant discovery forced them off the ship. "I'm sorry, Fitz," she said.

Jem turned the tube over in his hands. "It's all right." He raised it to his eye and pointed it toward the growing blot on the horizon.

"What do you see?" Scarlet asked, not really wanting to hear the answer.

Jem handed her the spyglass. "Look for yourself."

She pressed one eye up to the glass and waited for her vision to adjust. When it did, she saw the unmistakable shape of a schooner rising and falling with the waves. She found its mainmast, then followed it up to the ship's flag. It took her a moment to decipher the shape on the flag, but soon she recognized the profile of the Dread Pirate Captain Wallace Hammerstein-Jones flapping in the breeze. Scarlet rolled her eyes and handed the tube back to Jem. A sea monster would have been a much more welcome sight.

"It's them," she told her friends. "They're following us."

"Figures," Tim muttered.

"How much longer till we get to Island X, Swig?" Scarlet asked.

"A good hour, I'd say," he replied, gnawing on his lower lip. "They're bound to close in on us before we get there."

Scarlet sighed. That blasted Lucas Lawrence. And to think she'd lost sleep worrying that a horde of wild pigs had ripped him limb from limb. If only it had. She should have keelhauled him herself while she had the chance. And worst of all, he'd taken their map! She punched her right fist into her left palm and shouted, "All hands on deck!"

In minutes, the Lost Souls all stood before her, casting nervous glances over their shoulders at the approaching schooner.

"All right, crew. We won't have much time once we reach the shores of Island X, so let's get organized now. We need to think of some way to scare off the pirates before they can get inland. We need a . . . a . . ."

"A preemptive strike," Jem offered.

"Right. Or just a quick way to scare the trousers off 'em. Any ideas?"

The Lost Souls looked at one another and shrugged.

"I've got a jolly dagger." Elmo held up his weapon.

"Ever used it, though?" Liam asked.

"Well, no. But it looks kind of deadly."

"The *Dark Ranger* pirates have every weapon from the cutlass to the cannon," Tim reminded him. "A dagger or two won't exactly send them running." The Lost Souls looked at their weapons in doubt.

"All right then." Scarlet tried another tactic. "What're pirates most afraid of?"

The crew fell silent again. Then Ronagh spoke up. "That's easy. The islands. Remember Cutthroat MacPhee?"

"Cutthroat MacPhee. Hmmm . . ." Scarlet studied her cabinmate for a moment. "The islands. Hmmm . . ." Then she nodded. "That's it, Ronagh. The islands. Exactly."

From her perch in a sturdy tree where the beach met the jungle, Scarlet could see the *Dark Ranger* pirates rowing to shore. She gulped and lowered Jem's uncle's spyglass. There were probably fifty of them—more than twice the number of Lost Souls. Could they really pull this off? She raised the spyglass again.

The first boat held her two biggest nemeses, Lucas Lawrence and Captain Wallace. They were pointing and discussing something with two other men—Iron "Pete" Morgan, with the tight, red head scarf, whom she'd tied up on the *Dark Ranger* just hours ago, and a gigantic pirate with a face like a Saint Bernard. They were probably debating where best to enter Island X's dark jungle and how to find the trail the Lost Souls had cut through it mere days ago. Or perhaps they were wondering where the Lost Souls had disappeared to after anchoring the *Margaret's Hop* and rowing to shore. Scarlet hoped her crew was hidden well enough. She hugged the tree trunk and looked to her right, where Tim straddled his own branch. He winked back.

The *Dark Ranger* pirates kept their wary eyes on the trees as they sloshed through the shallows and up onto the beach. Most had their weapons drawn and ready. Scarlet gulped again and trained the spyglass on Lucas's face. His expression was grim, but his furrowed forehead gave away his uncertainty. She hoped his conscience was killing him, the bilge rat.

"Thomas, out in front!" Captain Wallace yelled out. "Use your cutlass to clear the jungle and make way for the rest of us!"

The poor Saint Bernard looked like his master had just declared him fit to be put down, but he gripped his weapon and inched toward the trees. Lucas followed close behind.

"Almost there," Scarlet whispered under her breath. "Almost there. And . . . *now*."

The smallest Lost Souls, hiding in the bushes near the edge of the jungle, started up their chorus. First came Sam's breathy moan, then a few eerie notes from Liam's flute, followed by Ronagh's cackling laughter. The pirates froze and exchanged glances, which turned from uneasy to terrified as a few other Lost Souls threw in some ghoulish shrieks. Thomas turned, ready to flee, but Captain Wallace, who'd been cowering in the big man's shadow, stopped him with a slap to his chest.

"Don't even think about it, Thomas. It's . . . it's just the wind. D-don't tell me you're af-f-fraid."

Just then, Ronagh screamed like a banshee, and the captain nearly clambered into Thomas's arms.

"It's just them—the crew I told you about," Lucas

said with a scowl. "They're trying to scare us. I know it. Keep going."

So he did tell them after all, Scarlet thought. *So much for the legend of the Lost Souls.*

"S-someone else go first," Thomas said. "Cap'n, you go. I think this is one of *those* islands."

"What?" Captain Wallace took a step back. "I can't go first. I . . . I get claustrophobic. Small spaces, you know."

"Oh, I'll go." Lucas stepped up, looking disgusted. "There's nothing to be afraid of."

Scarlet looked over at Tim and raised her hand in signal. Time for Phase Two of Operation: Petrify the Pirates.

She let Lucas pass underneath the tree, but when Captain Wallace's head came into view below her, she lowered a long vine until it just tickled his scalp.

The man screamed. "Snakes! Oh God, I hate snakes!"

Behind him, Iron "Pete" Morgan yelped when Tim's "snake" smacked his head scarf. Then all the Lost Souls hidden in the trees dropped their snake-vines at once, making the pirates duck and holler. Some, including Captain Wallace himself, started to run back toward the shore, but once again Lucas yelled for them to stop.

"They're just vines, not snakes. What kind of pirates are you?"

"Just wait, Lucas Lawrence," murmured Scarlet. "Time for Phase Three." She gave the signal—a parrotlike squawk—and ten more Lost Souls burst out of the trees, roaring like wild beasts and waving their arms. Except they were no longer Lost Souls. In less than fifteen minutes, Jem and his crew had outfitted themselves in ferns of every shape and size, and smeared dirt all over their faces. They wielded long fern-swords and wore leaves in their knotty hair. Looking down on them, Scarlet decided they were the most convincing island fiends she could ever imagine.

Apparently, Captain Wallace and his pirates agreed. All at once, they turned and ran, hollering, back to their rowboats, with Thomas and the captain leading the way. Lucas ran with them but slowed to a jog when he reached the sand. Scarlet waited until he was a fair distance away to leap down from her perch onto the forest floor, where the island fiends were already slapping one another on the back and laughing.

"It worked!" Elmo turned a cartwheel.

"Did you see their faces?"

"We've got them on the run," said Smitty.

"But not for long," Scarlet added. "They'll be back, and soon, if Lucas has anything to do with it."

"What happens next, then?" Gil Jenkins asked. He'd been one of the island fiends, and in the excitement seemed to have forgotten his loyalty to the one who'd defected.

Over on the beach, Lucas, Captain Wallace, and Pete were all shouting and gesturing madly to the trees.

"I think we're going to have to split up," Scarlet said. "We'll need one crew to stay and scare the pirates as long as they can and another crew to go on ahead to find the treasure." She chose a group to accompany her and

Jem on the treasure hunt and put the others in charge of scuttling Lucas's plans. A few Lost Souls looked disappointed to be left behind, but most took up their posts with an air of importance. Scarlet instructed them to follow her trail only when the coast was clear.

"And may you die peacefully in your hammocks rather than . . ." She glanced toward the pirates. Now probably wasn't the time. "Ah, forget it. Just go scare those scalawags silly."

Then she turned to Jem, Tim, Smitty, Liam, and Ronagh, who awaited her direction. Together, they plunged into the jungle, back on the treasure trail.

CHAPTER SEVENTEEN

The voice returned, not twenty steps into the jungle. It flooded Scarlet's brain with moans and whispers and words she couldn't decipher, yet again. She stopped and shook her head; she'd forgotten about this part.

"What's up?" Liam peered around her, probably expecting another angry monkey.

Scarlet almost told them all, right there. But she lost her nerve. What would she say, anyway? "There's this creepy voice in my brain, see . . ."

"Nothing," she said—a bit too forcefully, for Liam looked startled—then continued down the trail.

They moved faster this time, since the trail had been cut and trampled already. As they hiked, they reminded one another not to touch the trees, make eye contact with the animals, or look up at the poisonous canopy.

But Jem, still wearing his island fiend costume of ferns and dirt, kept glancing behind. And they hadn't been walking for more than twenty minutes when he uttered a foreboding, "Oh no."

"Don't like the sound of that, mate," Smitty commented without turning around. He hiked in a similar outfit, with a wig of curly ferns cascading down his back.

"They're coming," Jem said in a shaky voice. "Look."

The others turned. Sure enough, Scarlet saw a flash

of red not fifty yards back down the trail and heard the shing of a cutlass through some ferns.

"Oh *no*." Tim could only echo Jem's reaction.

"Run" was the only solution Scarlet could come up with. "As fast as you can. We'll try to lose them."

They didn't stop running until they reached the point at which the trail began to climb, where they paused to catch their breath.

"Think we lost 'em?" Ronagh panted.

"Doubt it. The trail's easy to follow, and even if they're stupid enough to lose it, they've got our map," Tim said.

Scarlet looked up at the switchbacks that rose above them, remembering the unpleasant climb. But at least it wasn't raining. Yet.

They scampered on, up the mountainside, over fallen trees, under vines that reached for them like tentacles, mindful of the millipedes that pattered along the amber earth and of every rustle in every bush. Scarlet took to chanting, "Shut up, shut up," to the voice that plagued her brain, but it only got louder the higher they climbed.

When the tree canopy finally thinned to reveal a pale gray sky, the Lost Souls collapsed on the dirt, wheezing. They'd reached the ridge.

"Where's . . . where's the spyglass?" Jem gasped. Smitty drew it out of his sleeve and handed it over. Jem pointed the tube down the hill and squinted into it. After a moment, he lowered the instrument.

"They're still coming. But we've put some distance between us."

"Let me see." Scarlet stood and reached for the tube. At first she saw nothing but jungle, but soon she caught several movements among the trees. The giant Thomas marched in front, holding his cutlass like a shield before him. Next came Lucas's dirty nest of brown hair, his face buried in the map. Captain Wallace followed, windmilling his arms at every insect he saw. Last came Iron "Pete" Morgan, looking exasperated with the whole mission.

"How can we lose them?" Liam asked.

Scarlet lowered the spyglass and bit her lip. She didn't have an answer, except, "Let's just keep going as fast as we can."

Then she remembered that this was the place that called for Jem's plant identification skills. Apparently he remembered, too, for he suddenly looked nervous.

"'Left at the *Abicatus florificus*,'" he recited. Mouth set in a hard line, he began to search every inch of the ground.

Scarlet looked over her shoulder now and then, tempted to ask Jem politely if he could hurry it up. But she kept her mouth shut. They couldn't afford a wrong turn again.

Finally, Jem settled on the same fuzzy stalk with the bushy, pink head he'd pointed out the first time. He stared at it for a while as if that might make the plant wake up and say, "Oh, dear me, yes, it's this way." But nothing happened, and Jem shrugged. "I'm fairly positive this is it. Maybe eighty-five percent certain this time. All right, eighty-two."

Scarlet nodded. "Then let's go. Come on, crew. You remember the way down."

They did. Smitty led the way, sliding down the hillside

on the mat of ferns he'd worn only moments before. The others followed suit, and though the ride was just as exciting as the time before, albeit a little less muddy, the urgency of the chase kept them from shouting in glee as they hurtled down, down, down the slope.

Scarlet, however, found her own ride much less pleasant this time thanks to the voice that, despite her chanting, simply refused to shut up. By the time the Lost Souls had picked themselves up off the grass at the foot of the slope and began running through the Valley of Simmering Streams, she didn't know if she could take it anymore. The moans and drones would drive her crazy if she didn't do something about them.

"Stop!" she yelled finally, and the group came to a surprised halt near a little river that bubbled like clam chowder on the fire.

"Right," Jem said. "We've got to decide which way to go. We took a wrong turn somewhere around here last time."

"It's not just that," Scarlet said miserably. "I'm hearing a voice."

"A voice? What kind of voice?" Tim said.

"I don't hear anything." Ronagh wrinkled her nose.

"That's just it," Scarlet wailed. "No one else hears it. It's plagued me ever since I first set foot on this island, moaning and whispering like nothing I've ever heard, and I can't take it anymore. What do you do with a voice that just won't shut up?"

"Um . . . listen to it?" Smitty suggested with a nervous smile. "Maybe it's got something to say."

Scarlet stopped and looked at him.

"Sorry. Weak attempt at humor." Smitty hung his head. "It's not the time or place, I know."

Suddenly, Scarlet heard another voice in her head: *You've just got to listen,* Ben had said. *Listen to the people around you, but more importantly listen to yourself. All the answers you need are there.*

And so, as the others looked on, Scarlet sank to her knees on the earth and squeezed her eyes shut.

"Um, Captain, now might not be the best time for a rest," she heard Smitty say. Someone shushed him. Scarlet tuned them out and tuned in to the voice—its undulating moans, its urgent whispers. *I might have all the answers I need to understand this,* she thought, *but I'm going to have to dig deep for them.*

She tuned into herself, searching for a place deep inside where answers might exist. She scanned the dustiest shelves of her brain and perused the darkest corners of her memory. She searched deeper, until she felt like she had reached her core, where the essence of Scarlet flickered as it had since the day she was born. She knew this was the place, for she felt completely at home.

Scarlet opened her eyes.

The scene before her looked different somehow. Vapor still rose from the simmering streams, the sky overhead was still the same pale gray, and the Lost Souls still stared at her as if she'd grown another nose, but somehow, everything looked a little more familiar. A little more clear. Or maybe it was just her, feeling a little more . . . herself.

She looked to her left, toward a patch of trees that wavered like a mirage. A ribbon of red wove through them—an ara, Scarlet was certain. She stared harder at the trees until she saw a path materialize between them: a narrow but well-worn path she'd never seen before.

"It's that way." She pointed for her friends, who looked bewildered.

"How do you know? I don't even see a trail." Smitty squinted in the direction she pointed.

"I just know." Scarlet clambered to her feet. "You were right. I listened, first to the voice, then to myself. I found the answers."

Now the Lost Souls looked certain she'd gone off the deep end.

"Scarlet, are you—" Ronagh began in a whisper.

"Oh no. Look." Jem pointed up the hill, where Lucas was preparing to barrel down on his rear end while the other pirates exchanged dubious looks.

"You've just got to trust me," Scarlet said to her friends. "Please. I won't let you down. I *know* this is the way."

Lucas was now tumbling at top speed toward them. "I'm in," Liam said. "Let's go." The others nodded.

"Wait," said Tim. "We can't all go. If the pirates see us all heading that way, they'll just follow. But if we split up, if several of us go the wrong way, we could head them off then catch up later."

The Lost Souls looked at one another and nodded again, just as Lucas's cry soared over the steam: "I see them! Hurry up! We have to catch them!"

"You and Jem go on ahead," Tim ordered. "The rest of us'll take 'em on a wild chase. We'll catch you later."

Scarlet began to protest—what if the path didn't appear for her friends? But something deep inside told her that it would. And she trusted it.

"Good luck." She grabbed Jem's arm and started running toward the patch of trees, where the path still shimmered before her, inviting them in.

"Fitz," she puffed as they hurried along the twisting dirt trail.

"Hmm." He hadn't said much since she'd pulled him into the trees and the jungle closed behind them like a door. But then, what could she expect? Even she had to admit that mysterious voices, magical paths, and pirates in hot pursuit could overwhelm a person unused to such things.

"You never told me what your uncle thought the treasure is."

Jem nodded. "You're right. After all this time."

"Well?" Scarlet stopped, glanced behind her to make sure no one was following them, then looked at Jem.

"Well, have you ever heard of a bromeliad?"

Scarlet shook her head.

"A bromeliad's a type of plant. They're . . . um . . . epiphytic. That means they grow attached to other plants, but don't harm them." He looked proud to have remembered that knowledge. "Uncle Finn spent years researching bromeliads here on the islands. Dead, boring stuff, if you ask me, but somewhere along the way, he decided that the treasure is actually a bromeliad with healing powers. Kind of like Liam's salve, I suppose."

Scarlet was quiet for a minute, trying to picture this and wondering how it fit with her own theory. Then she started to laugh.

"What?" Jem immediately turned defensive. "Oh, and I suppose a magic bromeliad is so much funnier than a magic spice?"

"It's not that." Scarlet giggled. "It's that . . . just think how mad Lucas would be if he knew he was on the trail of some old plant rather than a chest full of jewels. Can you imagine his face?"

Jem's own face broke into a grin, and he let out a hoot. "You're right. He's in for a surprise. If Uncle Finn's theory is correct, that is. To be honest, though, I can't help but hope it's something more exciting than a plant. Smitty's golden conch—now that sounds jolly."

"Come on. Let's keep going." Scarlet started off again down the path with Jem close behind. "There're so many theories," she said as they hurried along, "and really, any one of them could be right." The suspense was practically killing her. She picked up the pace around the next bend in the path. "Is it just me, or is it getting ridiculously hot?"

Suddenly, the trees parted, and Scarlet and Jem found themselves looking down into a lake. A great, big, steamy crater lake the milky, blue-green color of the sea where it met the sand. They stopped, then turned to each other with wide eyes.

"The boiling lake!"

"The real thing this time!" Without thinking, Scarlet threw her arms around Jem's neck. Then, realizing how positively uncaptainly that was, she took a hasty step back. Jem looked a little flushed, but it could have been the temperature. His shirt was soaked with sweat underneath his leafy overcoat.

They paused for a few moments, sweating and staring down the clifflike walls surrounding the boiling water, wondering how the lake had ever come to be. Then Jem wiped his forehead and shrugged. "Well. We're on the right path. No sense stopping here."

On they marched, following the trail as it twisted to the right, away from the lake and into a much cooler and shadier forest.

"Can you picture the map in your head, Fitz?" Scarlet asked as they walked.

"A little. I wish I'd studied it closer when Uncle Finn and I were traveling. I always figured I'd have him to guide me, or at least the map itself."

"I don't remember much, either. Something tells me we're approaching one of those landmarks, though."

The forest seemed to grow darker the farther they went. By Scarlet's calculations, it couldn't be later than midday; surely the sun wasn't setting yet. But it was getting more difficult to distinguish shapes from shadows, and the trees seemed to be closing in, making the path even narrower and the jungle even more impenetrable.

Suddenly, the ground dropped off right in front of them, and Scarlet stumbled backward, treading on Jem's toes as she scrambled away from the edge.

"It's . . . it's a pit of some sort," Jem said, peering down. "I can see the path climbing out of it on the other side. It's no more than four or five yards across."

Scarlet didn't feel reassured. She had no desire to climb into a deep, dark pit inhabited by who knew what, even if the path did continue on the other side. Recalling the stories of men who'd ventured into the jungle never to be seen again, Scarlet rejected the idea of straying off the path, especially since it seemed to want to show her the way. If only they could consult the map to—

"Wait. Fitz, didn't the map say something about an o . . . ophid . . . oh, what was that word?"

"An ophidian aggregation!" Jem exclaimed. "Scarlet, that's it!"

"What's it?"

"That's the word I was looking for days ago. The one that describes a . . . oh *no*."

"Seriously, Jem, these 'oh nos' are getting a little tiresome. What's an ophid . . . you know?"

"A . . . a writhing mass of snakes."

Scarlet's lower lip sagged. "You mean like . . ."

"The one that killed Cutthroat MacPhee."

"Oh *NO*."

They peered into the pit again, and sure enough, even in the dimmest light, Scarlet could see something wriggle. Then something else. Yes, the entire pit was slowly moving with lithe, scaly bodies. She took a step back. "I can't."

"Wait." Jem put a hand on her arm. "Remember Tim's story. The snakes had no intention of killing Cutthroat MacPhee. He died of fright."

"Who can judge a snake's intentions?" Scarlet wailed, more for the sake of stalling than argument. "And, anyway, if the world's most bloodthirsty pirate fell victim to an ophidiwhatsit, then how can we expect to get by? We're just children."

As soon as the words left her mouth, Scarlet wanted to kick herself. The Lost Souls would be so disappointed in her.

Jem shook his head. "I won't tell anyone you said that if you cross this pit right now."

Scarlet drew a breath. She'd go barefoot through the pit if it would erase the uncaptainly thing she'd just said. "Let's go." Without another moment's hesitation, she stepped off the edge and let the crumbling earth carry her down into the pit.

The first step was the worst. The snakes shuddered and wound themselves around her boots, then climbed up her calves. There were hundreds, even thousands of them piled on top of one another, and Scarlet was glad for the dim light that kept Jem from identifying their species and telling her how deadly they were.

The second step was almost as bad. One damp, cool body slipped inside her boot and wrapped itself around her ankle. Another climbed farther, to the soft spot behind her knee. Their hissing grew louder, like a chorus in her ears. Their bodies rippled and swelled like waves—a sea of dark, clammy, wriggling . . .

She closed her eyes and searched for an answer to the question: Is this really necessary?

Something deep inside told her that she'd pass

unharmed. Scarlet sighed. She supposed she could take a little trauma. Maybe she even deserved it after what she'd said about them being "only children."

They waded through what seemed like miles of squirming bodies but was really only a few yards before the trail began to climb out of the pit. The snakes loosened their hold on Scarlet's legs and let her scramble, unscarred, up onto the ledge.

She pulled a straggler out of her boot, tossed it into the pit, and turned to Jem. "That was disgusting."

He nodded. "I didn't want to tell you back there, but we just waded through a pit of deadly striped vipers, some of the most venomous snakes around."

Feeling ill, Scarlet glanced back at the pit. "This had better be one good treasure."

Once they'd passed the snake pit, the tree canopy began to thin, and a bit of sunlight streamed in through the cracks. Scarlet and Jem began to chant one of Smitty's chanteys to keep themselves moving.

> *There may be snakes in every tree*
> *And spiders on the ground,*
> *But how could we stay home when there's*
> *A treasure to be found?*
>
> *March, two, three, four.*
> *March, two, three, four.*

Although they were still far from safe, Scarlet was feeling more relaxed now that the deadly striped vipers were behind them. She could tell that Jem felt it, too, and was about to teach him a new, crusty pirate tune when she smelled it.

"Scurvy. What is that?" she asked, pinching her nose.

"Well, you know what they say, Cap'n," Jem replied. "He who smelt it, dealt it."

"Shut up, Fitz. I'm serious. That is *rank*."

Then they heard it: first one rustle in the bushes, then another, and another. Followed by a soft *click-clack*, like small hooves on pebbles.

Rustle click, rustle clack.

Then they saw it: an army of dark beasts slipping out of the trees and onto the trail. No taller than dogs, but round like rum barrels, the creatures pressed their snouts into the amber earth and fixed their glinting eyes on the two Lost Souls.

"Scarlet," Jem whispered.

"Uh-huh."

"Tell me those aren't what I think they are."

But Scarlet could think of no other island inhabitants that could be mistaken for smelly wild pigs.

CHAPTER EIGHTEEN

"Maybe if you listened again," Jem said as they slowly backed away from the snorting hogs, "you'd find the answer to: What on earth do we do now?"

"Maybe," Scarlet replied without taking her eyes off the pigs. "But I think it'd take some concentration. I might have to close my eyes and even sit down."

"And it's really not the best time for that, is it?" Jem snapped. Against his better judgment, he'd trusted in Scarlet's mysterious knowledge of the island. But where was that knowledge now that they were staring down the ugliest, smelliest creatures he'd ever come across? The pigs reeked like some combination of onions, dog breath, sweaty socks, and old cheese. Except worse—much, *much* worse. They had mottled, gray skin and were bald except for a few long, black hairs on their snouts and between their eyes. They lumbered rather than walked, with a side to side swagger reminiscent of drunken pirates in port, and their teeth poked out of the corners of their mouths, glinting like tiny daggers.

This adventure had just reached new heights of absurdity—not ten minutes after crossing a pit of venomous vipers, here they were being stared down by a pack of putrid pigs that wanted to rip them limb from limb. And all for a treasure that may well turn out to be a plant? It didn't make a speck of sense. Desperate for logic, Jem resorted to asking himself, "What would Master Davis—"

But before he could even finish the question, one of the larger boars seemed to decide enough was enough and charged straight for them. With his snout in the dust and his tusks aimed right at Jem's knees, the boar galumped forth, full speed, then came to a grunting halt a hair's width from Jem's trousers.

Scarlet let out a loud sigh of relief. The boar grunted and swung its head from side to side. Jem clutched his whomping heart. Master Davis didn't matter anymore. Jem had to find his own way out of this, playing by the islands' rules of logic.

Think fast, he told himself. *What are these pigs so upset about?*

That was easy—they saw him and Scarlet as a threat. The islands had been invaded time and again, their homes torn up in an endless search for wood, spices, and jewels. Maybe the King's Men even hunted them for food, like they did back in the Old World.

He would have to show the pigs he meant no harm. But how?

"What," Jem asked himself without taking his eyes off the angry boar before him, "would Master Davis never, ever do?"

The answer that came to mind sounded so absurd, it made perfect sense.

"Scarlet."

"Uh-huh."

"I think we're going to have to talk to them."

"Talk," she repeated, then turned to stare at Jem.

"Yes."

"To the pigs."

"Right."

"Because you think they'll understand us." She couldn't have looked more baffled if he sprouted a snout himself.

"Just because you've never met a pig that understands English doesn't mean they don't exist." He dared to grin at her, well aware that under different circumstances the remark would have earned him a smack upside the head.

Then he turned to the pig who was drooling on his shoe.

"First of all, let me say that we mean no harm. We don't want to hurt you or any of your friends, and certainly not your home. We're here to make as little noise and as few footprints as possible. We're just going to take a look around for a treasure, then go back the way we came."

The pig turned its great head to one side and regarded Jem with what looked like suspicion.

"Besides, we've come so far already. Perhaps you could just let us pass this once. We'll be no trouble, I promise. You have the word of a Lost Soul."

That last bit seemed to clinch it. The pig gave a final grunt, swung around, and trundled off with his band, leaving Scarlet and Jem one last whiff of his nasty odor.

They stood frozen moments after the smelly wild pigs had disappeared.

"Fitz," Scarlet finally gasped. "You did it. You spoke

to a smelly wild pig and . . . and he listened. To *you*!"

Even Jem couldn't believe what he'd done. He only knew that no one back home could ever hear of it. And he was fine with that.

"Have you noticed how much brighter the forest has gotten?"

"And louder. Listen to those bird songs."

They'd barely scurried a mile past the pigs when the scenery began to change.

"Is it just me or does the air smell sweet?"

"I think it's warmer, too. Do I hear water? Is that a creek?"

Two steps more and they had to stop to take it all in. It was the most beautiful sight Jem had ever seen.

The trees had parted to reveal a clearing shaped like a perfect circle, bordered by high palms and giant ferns. Inside the clearing stood shrubs covered in flowers of every color; Jem recognized several from the *Pseudophoceae* family, among Uncle Finn's favorites. In the very center of the clearing, a creek spilled softly into a shining pool, also perfectly round and perfectly clear. Two ruby-red birds sailed across the sky and disappeared into the trees.

The air smelled spicy-sharp and sweet at once. But there was something else in it—a feeling. A peaceful, contented sort of feeling.

Try as he might to stay focused on uncovering the treasure before the pirates caught up with them, Jem felt his anxiety ebbing like a lazy tide. He looked at Scarlet to see if she felt it, too. She was smiling in a way he'd never seen before. In fact, she was almost radiant, like the place itself.

"This place . . . ," she whispered without looking at him. "It's so beautiful. And . . . familiar?"

"Beautiful, yes." Jem watched his captain twirl around in a slow circle, looking dazed. "But I'm not sure about familiar." She certainly was acting odd, even for Scarlet.

Actually, she was looking more and more like she might collapse on the grass and go to sleep. Jem tried to fight his own urge to do the same. There was a treasure to be found. And the rest of the crew, of course. And . . .

"Jem!"

It had been only a week since Jem had heard that voice, but it felt like years. Decades, even.

Jem and Scarlet turned. Rappelling down a palm tree on the edge of the clearing was none other than the famed explorer Finnaeus Bliss. The man laughed as he slid down his rope and planted both feet on the forest floor.

Jem's jaw dropped. "Sink me!"

"I was starting to think you'd never get here!" Uncle Finn wiped the sweat from his bald head. "Whatever took you so long? I thought you'd be here ages ago, what with the map and all . . ."

Aside from being a few pounds lighter, Uncle Finn didn't look half bad, considering he was supposed to be dead.

"You're not dead!" Jem shouted as he ran for his uncle.

"Not yet!" Uncle Finn swooped him up in a great hug that left his nephew unable to breathe.

"Are you sure?" Jem gasped as he watched the world spin over his uncle's shoulder.

"Quite." Uncle Finn set him down. Jem latched onto his uncle's arm, both to ensure the man was real and not a ghost and to keep himself from falling over.

"But how?"

"I'll tell you all about it," Uncle Finn promised. "But first tell me what's happened to you. And don't forget to explain why you're dressed up like a *Podipus alpus*."

Jem drew a deep breath and spewed his story as fast as he could, dying to hear his uncle's own story of escape.

"So the long and short of it is, the pirates have the map and were hot on our heels last time we saw them," Jem concluded. His words suddenly reminded him that the rest of the crew might well be in danger and not far away. As comforting as this place felt, and as deliriously happy as he was to be reunited with his uncle, he couldn't forget them.

"Hurry, Uncle Finn. Tell us what happened to you."

"Well, you've obviously guessed that the pirates didn't make me walk the plank. I think it was a barrel they threw over in my place—just a ploy to get you to talk," Uncle Finn began. "They did, however, tie me up, gag me, and throw me in a very uncomfortable, dark space where I had no hope of alerting you. I thought we were through, both of us"—he reached out to lay a sap-

219

covered hand on Jem's hair—"but then one of the pirates had a change of heart."

"What? Which one?"

"Thomas, the one with Herculean shoulders. He said the guilt was eating away at him, especially since you'd been kidnapped by a bunch of deadly ghosts." Uncle Finn smiled. "Oh, it's not that I wasn't worried for you. I was. But, well"—he paused, looking a little smug—"for the record, I always suspected the Lost Souls weren't as deadly as everyone thought.

"Anyway, poor Thomas's conscience was killing him. So the next time we docked in port, a few days after you left with the Lost Souls, he smuggled me off the boat and left me in Jamestown, where I found a sailor willing to take me to this island for a few doubloons."

The story left Jem speechless. So old Thomas had had the nerve to defy the Dread Pirate Captain Wallace Hammerstein-Jones. Jem shook his head. *Thomas* was the real hero of the story.

"Jem, you didn't introduce me to your friend." Uncle Finn turned to Scarlet, who'd hung back just to watch and listen.

"Scarlet McCray." Scarlet extended a hand, then leaned forward and whispered, "Just for the record, I always suspected you weren't as dead as everyone thought."

Jem grinned. "Scarlet's the captain of the Lost Souls."

"Captain!" Uncle Finn bowed over Scarlet's hand, looking impressed. "Then I thank you for saving my nephew, Captain Scarlet McCray. His parents would have killed me if I'd lost him."

"All right, all right," Jem said, not wanting to think about anything to do with the Old World at the moment. "Let's get to the point. Are we here? Have we almost reached the treasure?"

"Treasure?" Looking amused, Uncle Finn spread his arms out to the sides. "Look around you, boy. Is this not treasure enough?"

Scarlet was getting that dreamy look again. She nodded.

"Wait a minute," Jem said. "We came all this way for . . . *this*? I mean, don't get me wrong, this is a beautiful place, but is it really the treasure?" He looked at Scarlet, who simply smiled.

"It's treasure enough for me," she said.

Uncle Finn eyed her for a moment. "Then you'll want to thoroughly explore this place. But it might have to wait. If I recall correctly there are some angry pirates out there. With a map leading them directly to us."

"Right. Of course." Jem nodded.

Uncle Finn looked back toward the trail. "They've got our map, and that's bad. But they're also after your friends, which could be worse. Because, let's face it, they're only children."

Finally Scarlet snapped to attention. "Not just *any* children," she protested. "Children who sail the seas. Children who brave bloodthirsty swabs and deadly jungle creatures without a second thought nearly every—"

"Agreed, Captain," Uncle Finn cut her off. "They're not just any children. But they still may need our help."

Scarlet thought for a moment, then nodded. "Agreed."

She looked around her, eyes lingering on one of the red birds that had emerged from the trees and perched nearby. "As much as I don't ever want to leave this place," she said, "I can't desert my crew. Not now. Or ever, for that matter."

Jem didn't relish the thought of reencountering all they'd come across on the way. Especially those awfully smelly pigs. But they couldn't leave the others.

"Count me in, too," Uncle Finn said, looking at the soft ferns and the shimmering pool almost hungrily. "We'll have your friends back here in no time."

With that, he started marching toward the path they'd come in on. Jem and Scarlet took one last look at the clearing, where everything felt safe. Then they turned to follow Uncle Finn back into the jungle, where anything could happen.

CHAPTER NINETEEN

First came the pigs. The reeking leader, who'd charged at Jem less than an hour before, burst out of the trees not long after the trio left the protected place. He grunted and shook his wrinkly gray head from side to side as his equally malodorous posse shuffled out of the bushes and assembled behind him. Scarlet thought the leader seemed almost exasperated, as if he wanted to say, "What's the matter with you people? You said you'd only pass once. I've had just about enough of being bothered by humans."

In fact, the more she watched him, the more certain she felt that this was exactly what the old boar was trying to tell them. But how could she know that? She couldn't speak Pig to save her lost soul. All she knew was that this smelly wild pig felt irritated—and she was feeling that irritation for him. It was the strangest thing.

"I'll handle this." Uncle Finn pulled a syringe full of green syrup out of his trouser pocket. "The fastest way to pass these beasts is to inject them with a potent solution of soothing herbs. It makes their eyes droop like sleepy babies." He made a dive for the pig chief, ready to sedate him with the mysterious concoction.

"Wait!" Scarlet yelled, startling them all. Uncle Finn missed his target, tumbled forward, and ended up injecting a large mushroom on the path. It turned purple with white polka dots and wilted immediately.

The pig looked from Uncle Finn to Scarlet and grunted. Scarlet knew instinctively that if he could speak, he'd say something along the lines of, "Take that, you clumsy, flat-footed, pasty-skinned human." She decided not to relay the message.

"Fitz," she said instead. "Talk to him like you did last time. Tell him we have to pass again to save our friends from some bad men who want to harm the island. Tell him we're acting in his best interests and we'll make sure no one damages his home."

Jem repeated the message as if he were standing before the throne of King Aberhard himself, while Uncle Finn looked on incredulously from where he still sat, legs splayed, in the middle of the path. When Jem finished his request with a polite bow, the pig grunted again—Scarlet was certain he'd have rolled his eyes if he could—and jerked his head to the right. His putrid posse shuffled back into the trees, leaving a rancid cloud for the trio to pass through.

"I . . . I can't believe it," Uncle Finn bumbled as Jem helped him to his feet. "You just spoke to one of the island's most deadly creatures. And . . . and it listened."

"I just told him what he needed to hear." Jem shrugged, but his ears were pink with pride.

They slipped past the wary chief, Uncle Finn still shaking his head in wonder. Scarlet was impressed with her friend's talents, too, but what concerned her most at that moment was her newfound ability to channel the island's feelings—or rather, the feelings of the island's inhabitants. Right then, she was picking up an uneasy sensation in the trees. She didn't know exactly which creature was feeling this, but she knew it was somewhere off to her left. Hiding.

She didn't have time to explore this phenomenon, however, because they were approaching her least favorite part of the trip: the ophid . . . ophidi . . . that *thing* full of deadly striped vipers. Scarlet turned to Uncle Finn. "I don't suppose you know any tricks to get us around the ophidiwhatsit?"

"The o-phi-di-an ag-gre-ga-tion," Uncle Finn said pointedly. "And who needs tricks? You simply follow the explicit instructions on the map: "Ophidian aggregation. Keep right. Or in this case, left."

"Keep right?" Scarlet repeated, then turned to Jem. "We just had to *keep right*?" she growled.

"Of course. How did you two get around it?"

"Um, we took the scenic route," Jem said.

Uncle Finn raised an eyebrow at them but didn't twitch a whisker when they approached the pit. They slogged through the jungle and passed without incident.

"I can't believe you made me walk right through that," Scarlet grumbled to Jem as they marched away from the pit.

Jem gave a cool shrug. "It wasn't so bad."

She felt like lopping off his ear.

Soon the temperature grew warmer and continued to rise. With it rose Scarlet's apprehension. The trees quivered above them. The millipedes burrowed in the amber earth below, hiding their heads from a danger they couldn't identify. Scarlet couldn't identify it, either—all she knew was that she had to find her crew and get them safely back to the protected place.

A thick curtain of steam drifted across the path, and the jungle opened up onto the edge of the boiling lake. They stopped and stared down at its milky, blue-green bubbling water.

"Look!" Jem pointed through the steam to the far edge of the lake. Scarlet squinted and could just barely make out a small figure across the lake. Then another, and two more. They were creeping hesitantly toward the boiling water. One wore what looked like a headdress of ferns.

"The crew!" Scarlet had never been so happy to see them, and she took off at a sprint around the perimeter of the lake.

The Lost Souls looked up to see their captain barreling around the edge of the blistering water and cried out in relief. Scarlet ran straight into the middle of them and tried to hug as many as she could at once.

"Where've you been? Did you find the treasure?" Ronagh cried.

"Who's that?" Monty pointed at Finn as the man ran up, huffing, behind Jem.

"That's my uncle," Jem said.

"Your uncle!"

"Did you find 'im at the treasure?"

"Did you find the *treasure*?"

"First tell us what happened to you," Jem insisted.

"But hurry," Scarlet said, glancing around her. "We can't stay here long."

Monty, still in costume, cleared his throat. "We scared 'em good, we did. We kept making creepy noises and dropping snakes and chasing those old pirates around the jungle until they couldn't take it anymore and turned tail. Well, most of 'em did. Lucas and three others, including the captain, ran on past. The rest of those big babies rowed right back out to the *Dark Ranger* and wouldn't budge. That's when we decided it'd be safe to follow you. We stayed a good distance behind Lucas and his gang."

"Good for you," Scarlet said.

"And as for *our* crew," said Liam, "we made sure Lucas and the others were following close enough behind us, then took 'em straight to that old lukewarm slough. They weren't looking at the map, and they followed us blind. Then we ran on, leading 'em in big circles and always ending up back at the lukewarm slough. The captain was so mad he almost lost his mind."

All the Lost Souls laughed, imagining it.

"While the *Dark Ranger* pirates were arguing and threatening to hang each other," Tim continued, "we made a run for it, straight to the place where Scarlet told us we'd find the path. Not only did we find the path, but we found the rest of the crew. You were right, Cap'n—the path appeared like it'd always been there, and we've been following it ever since."

"So you're sure you lost the *Dark Ranger* pirates?"

"Fairly certain," Smitty said. "Now what's your story, Cap'n? Fitz? Fitz's uncle?"

Jem and Scarlet exchanged sly glances. "Let's just say . . . ," Jem began.

"We've got something to show you," Scarlet finished.

"What? What is it?" Ronagh squealed.

"Shh," said Scarlet. "Not now. We've got to keep moving. I just have this feeling . . ."

"But I can't stand the suspense," Ronagh whined.

"You'll see soon enough," Jem said, steering the younger girl back the way they'd come and beckoning the others to follow.

"Just give us a hint," Emmett pleaded.

"Is it big? Is it shiny?" Edwin persisted.

"Look, you'll know soon enough. Just follow quickly and quietly. I've got a bad feeling about—"

"STOP. RIGHT. THERE."

The Dread Pirate Captain Wallace Hammerstein-Jones's voice sliced through the steam like a cutlass through a thief's finger. The Lost Souls and Uncle Finn turned as a veil of steam lifted to reveal the rodentlike captain and his disheveled crew. Lucas, his face slippery with sweat and crisscrossed with scratches from unruly tree branches, looked triumphant. Iron "Pete" Morgan looked perplexed. Thomas the giant looked like he might cry.

"Look!" Captain Wallace cried. "Why, they're . . . they're only *children*."

"Course they are," said Lucas. "That's what I kept telling you."

"Yes, but"—Captain Wallace inched forward as if he were approaching wildlife that might be easily startled—"I didn't believe it. Imagine. The Ship of Lost Souls, a ship of . . . children." He stopped and began to laugh—a high-pitched, nasal cackle. Lucas joined in with forced chuckles, and Pete added a few halfhearted *har*s. Thomas's lower lip quivered.

"Well, this'll be easy." Captain Wallace wiped his forehead and took another step forward. "Getting to the treasure will be no challenge at all. Why, it'll be like taking candy from . . . children." He cackled again.

Scarlet rolled her eyes. She'd had quite enough. She stepped forward, motioning for the others to get behind her. "Captain Wallace," she said in her most commanding voice, "the children you see before you aren't just *any* children. These are children who sail the seas. Children who brave bloodthirsty swabs and deadly jungle creatures without a second thought nearly every—"

"Silence!" cried Captain Wallace. He licked the sweat off his upper lip. "Do I look like I *care*? I've got a blasted treasure map here, and I'm not going to let a bunch of half-pint-pirates stand in my way. Now get off the path and let us *real* pirates cross before we toss you into that big lake. Good *Lord*, does anyone else find it infernally *hot* around here?"

"It's a *boiling* lake, Captain," Pete sighed.

"Which you'd know if you'd consulted the map," Uncle Finn muttered.

"Why Finnaeus Bliss!" Captain Wallace's eyes lit up, noticing the man for the first time. "You old scoundrel. Thought you were so smart to escape my ship, didn't you? And here you are, hoping a bunch of children will protect you while I skip on past to collect my treasure. With your map! It's too funny! Ha-ha! Ha-ha!"

Now Scarlet had definitely had enough. She reached into her boot and drew out her dagger, took another swift step forward, and pointed it right between Captain Wallace's eyes. "Shut up," she said. "You'll never see the treasure. Not if I have anything to do with it."

For a moment, everyone froze. Then Jem moved to her side. "Or me."

"Me neither." Smitty stepped up behind them.

One by one, the Lost Souls and Uncle Finn took their places behind Scarlet and drew their weapons.

"W-what?" Captain Wallace sputtered. "What is this? You think you children are going to scare me off? You're crazy. You've got water on the brain. Thomas can crush you all at once. With his pinkie fingers. Go on, Thomas, take them out."

But the big man didn't move. He only looked at the Lost Souls with sad eyes.

"Thomas!" Captain Wallace screamed.

"Thomas," Pete whispered, nudging him. "Go on."

Finally Thomas took a step forward. He drew his cutlass and began to walk toward Scarlet. She gulped. She might be able to take on mousy old Captain Wallace, but a man Thomas's size? She didn't stand a chance.

But then, a few paces short, Thomas veered off. He walked straight toward the edge of the lake, stopped, and turned to face them. Swallowing hard, he held his cutlass out over the edge . . . and let it drop into the boiling water.

"I won't harm 'em, Captain," Thomas said softly as twenty-seven mouths dropped open. "These ain't just any children."

"You . . . you lout!" Captain Wallace sputtered. "Pete! Finish them off!"

Pete grasped his weapon and lunged for Scarlet. But he wasn't fast enough—for Thomas reached out and held the top of his shipmate's head in his big hand. "Sorry, Pete," he said, and continued to hold on tight while Pete tried to twist free.

"Oh, for Pete's sake." Captain Wallace stopped for a moment, distracted by his unintended pun. Then he screamed, "Lucas! Get them!"

"Which one?" Lucas yelled back with a tremble in his voice.

"The one who's pointing the dagger between my eyes, you stupid boy!"

"Oh." Lucas dove for Scarlet, who looked away from Captain Wallace just long enough to dodge her former crewman. Captain Wallace took advantage of the moment to draw his own cutlass and make a charge for Scarlet, but as he was about to pounce, Jem lunged, throwing all his weight into the captain's shoulder. They tumbled to the ground, and Uncle Finn, with a warrior's holler, threw himself on top.

Scarlet turned to face Lucas. The boy's lips were pressed into a hard line and his eyes showed no emotion. *How will this play out?* she wondered, gripping her dagger with sweaty fingers. Lucas looked like he wouldn't hesitate to slay her, but could she do the same to him?

He lunged, and she ducked to the right. The Lost Souls gasped and hopped out of the way. Scarlet turned to face her nemesis once again, trying to predict which way he'd lunge next. But as she watched his face for some indication, something in it began to change. His nose twitched and his eyes widened, locking on something behind her left shoulder. Scarlet heard a rustle and a rumble but didn't dare look back.

"What the flotsam?" she heard Tim breathe.

"What's going on?" shrieked Captain Wallace.

"And what is that *smell*?" Smitty added.

Lucas stood, frozen, and Scarlet finally dared a peek over her shoulder. There, behind her, behind the Lost Souls, stood the entire band of smelly wild pigs, shoulder to filthy shoulder, snouts in the dirt, grumbling what sounded like smelly pig swear words.

"Sink me," Scarlet whispered, turning to get a better look. She gasped as the ground beneath the pigs began to writhe with deadly striped vipers and the trees began to shake with dozens, scores even, of angry, hair-pulling monkeys. The vipers hissed and slithered closer. The monkeys muttered and waved whiplike vines.

"Captain, what do we do?" Edwin yelled.

"Nothing!" Scarlet answered without taking her eyes off the approaching army of wildlife. "I . . . I think they're on our side." *Oh God, I hope they're on our side,* she added to herself.

Sure enough, the leader of the smelly wild pigs picked Lucas out of the crowd and charged right for him. The boy hollered and took off running, followed by the pig chief and several monkeys turning wild somersaults. Uncle Finn and Jem let Captain Wallace scramble to his feet just as a group of aras swooped down from the treetops to dive-bomb him. The captain screamed and took off after Lucas, followed closely by Pete, a troupe of smelly wild pigs, and several dozen poisonous snakes. The animals brushed by Thomas but didn't harm him.

Scarlet stood and watched them go, her heart pounding. Then she turned to Jem, whose wide eyes, she guessed, were about the size of her own.

"They . . . saved us," he said. "But . . . how'd they know?"

Scarlet turned back to watch the rest of the snakes, pigs, and monkeys slinking back into the trees, their mission accomplished. She could sense the animals' relief. How *did* they know? The answer was slowly taking shape inside her head.

CHAPTER TWENTY

"So you're not satisfied with our treasure, are you, Jem?" Uncle Finn asked as he stretched out on the grass, running his fingers and toes through it.

"Well, it's not that." Jem, sitting cross-legged beside him, flushed. "I can see that this place is indeed quite the treasure. It's just . . . not what I expected."

Scarlet watched them, eyes half closed, from where she lay on her stomach beside the shining pool. All around her, the Lost Souls wandered as if in a dream, some exclaiming over star fruit and guava trees, some simply speechless at the beauty of the place. The traitor Thomas wandered with them. They couldn't desert him, after what he'd done. So what choice did they have but to bring him along? Now it looked like they might have an honorary crew member—or at least a new friend.

"Anyway," Jem said to his uncle. "It means you were wrong. The treasure isn't a magic bromeliad like you said. Or a magic spice, for that matter," he added, looking over at Scarlet.

"Hmm," she said, too preoccupied to argue. Hundreds of questions were crowding her brain, demanding answers right away. She had suspicions, inklings, and hopes, and she knew she'd have to look deep inside again for confirmation.

She retreated to her core, where she'd found answers

before, and began to sift through layers of memories, dusting off shelves of things forgotten. Images began to form in her brain, blurry at first, then gradually sharpening. She saw the clearing, but not as it looked now. A crowd of people. Islanders, she was certain, were milling around it, chatting as they dipped palm-leaf cups into the pool and drank its sparkling water. Others were sitting in the shade of the trees around its edge, munching on guava fruit, looking content. A group of barefoot children ran through, shrieking and laughing and tossing something red and shiny between them.

One small girl broke from the group and sprinted toward a willowy woman standing with friends on the edge of the pool. The woman dropped her basket of spices and gathered the girl in her long arms, then pointed to a flock of red birds sailing through the clearing. One briefly touched down on the ground and scraped the earth with its beak before taking flight again. The birds flapped off toward the trees and disappeared among them.

Scarlet sat up with a start. The damp grass had seeped into her shirt, which now clung to her cold skin.

"Well, I wouldn't say I was *wrong* exactly," Uncle Finn was grunting to Jem as he propped himself up on his elbow. "You see, there are indeed bromeliads around here, and they are indeed of the *Bediotropicanus* genus, and therefore by nature of their lineage and the structure of their cell walls, not to mention their propensity to flower when . . ."

Jem crossed his eyes at Scarlet and pretended to snore.

"I know where it is," Scarlet said.

"What? Know where what is?" Jem asked.

"Come on." And with that, she hopped to her feet and set off toward the trees. Jem and Uncle Finn only hesitated for a moment before stumbling after her.

"Where are we going?" Jem huffed as they waded through the bushes.

Scarlet came to a stop where her gut told her to. "Up."

"Up," Jem sighed. "Of course."

Scarlet grabbed the lowest branch and pulled herself up onto it. Then she reached for another, just above her head, and did the same thing again. Finally, she found the spot she was looking for: a thick, sturdy branch that could hold all three of them at precisely the right height. From there, she could look down on the entire clearing— the creek, the pool, and the ring of grass around it where the rest of the Lost Souls now sat cross-legged, enjoying the view. Jem swung himself up and settled beside her. Uncle Finn took a few more minutes, sweating and grunting not unlike the wild pigs on the trail.

"I hope you realize I'm not as young—" he panted.

"Look." Scarlet pointed to the next tree and to the one beyond it. Jem and Uncle Finn followed her finger. The branches held dozens of birds' nests, in which sat dozens of bright-red birds.

"Why, it's a rookery!" Uncle Finn exclaimed.

"It looks like a bunch of nests to me," Jem said.

Uncle Finn raised an eyebrow at his nephew. "If you'd been listening to the lectures, you'd know that a rookery is a nesting place."

"Oh. Right."

"At least tell me you recognize the bird."

Scarlet wanted to shout out the answer for everyone to hear, but she could tell Jem was thinking hard, recalling hours of lessons he'd dozed his way through. "An ara," he said finally. "Nearly wiped out by the King's Men when they first arrived here in the Islands."

"Exactly," Uncle Finn said. "A rare sight to see just one, but an entire colony!"

"Wait a minute," Jem said, leaning closer and squinting at the rookery. The aras eyed him, but didn't move. "Look at their nests. Are those . . ."

Scarlet grinned. Jem had found it. When the sun hit the nests at a certain angle, they began to twinkle with tiny bursts of red light, almost as if the sun were reflecting off hundreds of . . .

"Rubies?"

"Sink *me*," Uncle Finn whispered.

"Their nests are full of rubies?" Jem turned to her, wide-eyed. "But . . . how did you know?"

Scarlet took a deep breath and tried to explain. "I . . . looked inside me. And I discovered . . . or rather, I remembered. . . that is, you see . . . I'm home. Well, almost."

Jem and Uncle Finn exchanged confused looks while Scarlet gathered the nerve to admit what she hadn't said aloud in years.

"I'm an Islander. Well, half. My father was a King's Man who left his crew after falling in love with an Islander—my mother. Her people let him join them, and together they had me." She smiled uncertainly, amazed at how it was all returning to her now. "This clearing was a special place we all visited now and then, maybe a few times a year. It was a place where we felt safe and relaxed, where we could gather food and visit with friends and . . ." Scarlet closed her eyes, remembering the spices in her mother's basket and their wonderful smell, sharp and sweet at the same time. Then she opened her eyes and grinned. "And celebrate all the good things the island gave us."

"But . . . but," Jem sputtered, "why ever didn't you tell anyone?"

"Because I was told to forget," Scarlet answered. "And I forgot some things, or I tried to, since it hurt to think about it. When I was five, the Island Fever came through our village, and my mother asked my father to take me away while I was still healthy. She died of the fever after Father took me to Jamestown."

More memories flashed through Scarlet's brain. She saw the cool, palm-roofed hut where she had been forced to stay so she, too, wouldn't fall sick. She heard her neighbors' moans as, one by one, they began to cough, sweat, and succumb to the mysterious illness. She felt the good-bye kiss left on her forehead the night her mother sent Scarlet and Admiral McCray away. And the hot tears on her father's face as she clung to his neck while he tramped through the forest.

Home, she told herself, can't be far away. She wondered if the huts were still there, and what it would feel like to stand among them again.

Jem and Uncle Finn wore identical expressions of

bewilderment and grief. Scarlet looked away from them and back at the treasure. She smiled. "Look. No pirate or King's Man has ever found the source of the rubies, but the aras have known all along. They know exactly where to scrape the ground, nab a jewel here and there, and tuck them into their nests." She sighed. "Aren't they beautiful?"

"Then . . ." Jem squinted at her as if trying to make sense of everything he'd just learned. "This is the *real* treasure!" He bounced on his branch, then grasped it as he nearly lost his balance.

"Well, yes," said Scarlet. "And . . . maybe not. I think the Islanders saw the treasure differently. We played with the rubies as children—they weren't worth much to us. As long as we had land and food and family, we had everything we needed. In fact"—Scarlet wrinkled her nose, piecing it all together—"I bet old Admiral Angus thought the Islanders were keeping the rubies from him, when they were really here for the place itself."

Jem cocked his head, considering this. "So the *place* is the treasure. The rubies wouldn't be here if the animals and spirits hadn't protected it all these years."

"Or if the aras didn't collect them. That makes them a treasure, too," Scarlet added, then started as another memory was illuminated in her brain.

Uncle Finn, who'd been speechless until now, finally spoke. His voice sounded scratchy. "And these are the very birds they've all but killed off."

Scarlet nodded, feeling her own throat tighten. She stared at the red heads, and the birds gazed back, looking rather proud of themselves. Yes, that was it, precisely. She felt their pride. And at that, she began to cry.

"Scarlet, what's wrong?" Jem's face changed from delighted to concerned. He reached out through the foliage and patted her hand awkwardly.

"I'm sorry," Scarlet sniffled. "It's . . . it's the aras. I always knew . . . I mean, I'd forgotten . . ."

"What is it, dear?" Uncle Finn tore his eyes away from the birds and leaned forward on his branch to look at Scarlet as if examining a particularly unique specimen.

She bit her lip. "My real name is Ara. In my old language, it's a word for both the color—scarlet—and the bird. I'd forgotten until now." She wiped her eyes roughly with her sleeve. "After we left, my father stopped speaking my mother's language and started calling me Scarlet instead. I guess it hurt him to remember, too."

Jem looked like he wanted to speak, but instead he stayed quiet and held her hand.

Uncle Finn nodded thoughtfully. "This treasure—all of it, the place, the birds, the jewels—is badly in need of a guardian. Nearly every Old Worlder in the tropics would kill to get his hands on it. Certainly, it's protected by animals and spirits, but even those aren't invincible. We got past them, after all. And now that those pirates have the map, well . . ."

He gave Scarlet a meaningful look.

She bit her lip and nodded. Uncle Finn was right, of course. She'd known it ever since she realized she'd found her home. She'd certainly proven herself capable of leading the Lost Souls, but a guardian of Island X and all its treasures? Now *that* was a daunting job.

"I can't," she said.

"Why not?" Jem asked.

Scarlet shook her head. "I mean, not alone." Then she smiled at them. "This is a job for all the Lost Souls."

Jem drew a quick breath. He turned to Uncle Finn. "We can stay, right? At least for a while? I want to help."

Uncle Finn stroked the whiskers on his chin, pretending to mull it over. "You're in no hurry to get back to school, are you? Funny, that. Well, I do have a few hundred new bromeliad species to study." He smiled. "Of course we'll stay. For a while."

Jem punched the air in triumph. "Thanks, Uncle Finn. And, hey, I just thought of something. This treasure"— he gestured to the birds—"means that the legend is true. Rubies really *do* fall from the skies!"

Uncle Finn's mouth dropped open. Then he laughed. "So they do!"

Just then, a voice floated up from below, and the trio looked down to see a few Lost Souls staring up at them.

"What do you see up there?" Ronagh called.

"The view must be jolly from that height," Smitty said. "Can you believe this place? What a treasure!"

From their perch in the tree, Scarlet and Jem grinned at each other. What a treasure, indeed.

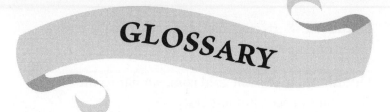

GLOSSARY

Amulet: an object worn, often as a piece of jewelry around the neck, to ward off evil

Blimey: an expression of frustration or surprise as in, "Remember when you dropped the anchor on my foot? Blimey, that hurt!"

Broadsword: a large, heavy sword with a broad blade

Buccaneer: a pirate. The term *buccaneer* comes from a French word (*boucanier*) which means "barbecuer." In the 1600s, buccaneers were humble men who sold barbecued meats to sailors passing through ports. Eventually they realized the opportunity passing them by and gave up their grills to make their fortunes by pillaging and plundering.

Careen: Cleaning the ship's hull involves beaching it, tilting it to one side, and scraping off the barnacles.

Castaway: a person lucky enough to survive a shipwreck and wash ashore, hopefully not on the Island of Smelly Wild Pigs

Crow's nest: the lookout platform near the top of a mast, not the best place for pirates afraid of heights

Cutlass: a short, curved sword with a single cutting edge, a pirate's best friend

Doubloon: a Spanish gold coin, similar to the chocolate variety, but less tasty

Drivelswigger: a pirate who spends too much time reading about all things nautical

Flotsam: floating debris or rubbish

Fo'c'sle: the raised part of the upper deck at the front of a ship, also called the forecastle

Gun deck: the deck on which the ship's cannons are carried

Jack-tar: a sailor

Keelhaul: the worst possible punishment on board a ship. The offender's hands are bound to a rope that runs underneath the ship, and he is thrown overboard and dragged from one end to the other.

Long drop: the Lost Souls' own term for the toilet

Mast: a long pole that rises from the ship's deck and supports the sails

Piece of eight: a Spanish silver coin

Plank: the piece of wood that hangs off the side of the ship, like a soon-to-be-dead-man's diving board. Unlucky sailors must walk it to their doom.

Plunder: to steal, or an act of thievery

Poop deck: the highest deck at the stern of a ship. It has nothing to do with the long drop, by the way.

Port: a sailor's word for *left*

Quarterdeck: the rear part of the upper deck at the front of a ship

Quartermaster: usually the second-in-command on a ship

Scalawag: a rascal, rogue, scoundrel, or general mischief-maker

Schooner: a ship with two or more masts. One explanation suggests that the name comes from the Scottish term "to scoon," which means "to skim upon the surface."

Scuttle: a word used by the Lost Souls to describe something awful as in, "Hardtack for breakfast again? That scuttles!"

Sloop: a small, single-mast ship

Spyglass: a much more intriguing name for a small telescope

Starboard: a sailor's word for *right*

Swain: a short form of *boatswain,* meaning a sailor of the lowest rank, more of a servant

ACKNOWLEDGMENTS

Many thanks to many souls. To my wonderful editors: Lynne Missen and Patricia Ocampo at HarperCollins Canada and Pamela Bobowicz at Grosset & Dunlap. To my agent, Marie Campbell, for believing in a ship of pirate children. To Alison Acheson, for feedback and encouragement throughout the first few drafts of the novel. To all who read thoughtfully and offered suggestions as the story changed course and shape, notably Louise Delaney, Sarah Dodd, and Allan Mott. To Tara MacDonald and her students at Greenview Elementary School, for dreaming themselves pirate. To Paul Colangelo, for cheering on the Lost Souls. To my family for unfailing support.

Photo by Shanna Baker

Rachelle Delaney lives in Vancouver, Canada, where she works as a writer, editor, and creative writing teacher. In 2010 she was named the top emerging writer in Canada by the Canadian Author's Association. *The Ship of Lost Souls* is her first novel.